1

"No!" Seefer Elliot shot up from his pillow holding his hands over his eyes. "I'll get up. I'll get up."

His mom walked away from the window having just thrown open the curtains. Seefer curled up in a ball trying to shield his blinded eyes. The sun's rays shined into his room with a brilliant luminosity.

"Please…my blanket…I need it."

Mom had pulled the blanket away five minutes earlier – her first attempt of getting him out of bed. Her maneuver proved to be unsuccessful and required a more convincing means of execution.

"Honey, if you were responsible enough to wake up the first time, I wouldn't be forced to use such cruel measures," she said. "You should learn to set your alarm."

"I did!"

Mom shot him a look of disbelief as she headed out the door.

"I really did! You never believe me." Seefer didn't understand how this could happen. He did actually set the alarm. *Was the volume on too low? Was it set for 7 p.m. instead of 7 a.m.?* He looked over at the clock on his nightstand. The power was on, but something was peculiar.

The hour slot flickered between *7* and *8*, while the minutes didn't look like numbers at all. Upon closer inspection, Seefer got a whiff of something burning. It smelled like a crayon melting on a radiator, not the most pleasant odor.

He mumbled, "Broken. See?" But his mom was nowhere near to behold the proof. There was no surprise in seeing yet another electronic device break in his house. It seemed to happen quite a bit lately.

Seefer remained in bed for a few minutes looking around his room. *I can't get up!* Posters of superheroes plastered his walls. *I bet their moms don't pry them out of bed for school.* While Seefer's interests weren't too peculiar for a 12-year-old boy, they often clashed with his schoolmates who'd rather follow their favorite sports teams instead of the latest adventures of Captain Quasar.

He flipped on the clock's radio switch. Luckily that function still worked. He had the radio set to a local rock station that pumped classics over the airwaves. He put his arms behind his head and enjoyed the moment

Seefer Elliot
and the World Aside Ours

Pat Mallon

of peace. *I could stay here all day.* His preference for these old rock anthems served as another point of contention between him and the other students who'd rather crank bubblegum pop through their ear buds.

His volatile relationship with his peers added to the many reasons that inhibited his excitement for school. Particularly a day like today. Not only was it a Monday, but a crisp November chill had set in. The house heat hadn't been turned on yet, so Seefer's blanket was his greatest comfort. Unfortunately, that was ripped away. To make matters worse, the clocks fell back the day before. His body hadn't adjusted well to waking up with the sun shining brightly before 6 a.m. *It's unnatural and cruel!*

At least one thing kept him looking forward to the day. Harrison Middle School would be hosting its annual Spirit Day, when fun activities and events would replace some of the mundane schoolwork. Since starting the 7th grade at Harrison, Seefer had been looking forward to it. All of the 8th graders talked about the amazing feats of last year's guests, the Percelli Brothers' Flying Acrobatic Circus. He hoped that this year's guest, Korvus the Magnificent, would top that. From the rumors going around, it looked like that would happen.

Students also were encouraged to wear the school colors, orange and grey. He found an outfit that fit the criteria and made his way down to breakfast.

Mom had his favorite cereal, Choco Balls, ready for

him on the table. He happily bounced into his seat while his mom scurried around the kitchen getting ready for her day. Something caught her eye that threw her off track. "Seefer?" She stared at him with a look of disbelief.

"What?"

"Weren't you wearing that stuff yesterday?" she asked knowing the answer.

"Yes?" he responded, not quite sure of the answer.

"Yes you were. Look at yourself. You are completely wrinkled. You have some kind of stain on the front of your shirt, soiled knees, and I'm sure if I came closer I would smell day-old socks."

Seefer looked at his outfit and realized that he may have made some oversights in his wardrobe choice. He had on his orange and black button down shirt tactically untucked from his grey cargo pants, but he missed the stains that his mom saw.

"But I have to wear these colors today. This is all I have."

"Seefer, I know you at least have one orange T-shirt somewhere. You have to start being more responsible. I shouldn't have to tell you that you look and smell like a railway hobo. And at your age, I shouldn't have to rip you out of bed."

"But my clock…"

"Blaming your lateness on an alarm clock is not going to fly with me. Was it your alarm clock that kept you up until eleven reading comic books?"

Seefer was caught off guard. *She knew about that?* "Sorry, Mom," he conceded.

"Never mind that. Hurry up so you can get new clothes on. You can't miss the bus this morning. I have a showing to get to before I pick you up for your doctor appointment."

"Doctor appointment?" he replied in disbelief. "But it's Spirit Day. I can't miss it."

"You won't miss much. It's just a quick check up. They have to keep tabs on you." She walked over and picked up the coffee pot. It was empty. "Ugh. Why doesn't anything work in this house?!"

Seefer slurped up his food quickly and ran out of the kitchen. He didn't want to be around his mom while she was mad *and* without coffee.

Seefer dug through his drawers looking for something wearable. He found the orange T-shirt his mom was talking about but soon realized she forgot that it was three years old, didn't fit him, and also had a popular children's cartoon drawn on it. Surely she was crazy for suggesting it.

He decided to change into some black pants and a grey T-shirt. He stuffed the stained orange button-down into his backpack, and hurried downstairs. He thought he would rub out the stain in the school bathroom and be good to go.

"Seefer! Let's go! You're going to miss the bus!"

He looked out the window and saw the bus in the distance. It never came to his house directly, so he had to stand at the end of the cul-de-sac in order to catch it. The town of Camden wasn't particularly good at providing its young residents with reliable transportation. This made for a huge inconvenience on days Seefer ran late.

He rushed downstairs and saw his mom standing at the open front door.

"C'mon!" She waved him through like a third base coach sending a runner home, then handed him a note. "Drop this off at the principal's office."

He landed a quick peck on her cheek and darted out the door in a full sprint. Bus 31 waited just past the stop sign at the end of the road. Not being the greatest athlete, Seefer found running an eighth of a mile a very difficult task this early in the morning. Today he was forced to race, his backpack flailing from side-to-side with each awkward stride.

As he ran past two houses, with two to go, he began to tire. "Wait for me!" he yelled. The bus driver didn't notice him; however, there were some kids at the back of the bus who could plainly see Seefer sprinting.

Seefer saw Hector Ramirez waving to the bus driver, reassuring him that no one was coming. He hated Hector and for good reasons such as this.

The bus driver, distracted by his obsessive cell phone use, ignored his duties and took the children's word that nobody was at the stop. He shut the door to the bus. Seefer, with only thirty yards to go, saw the devilish grin on Hector's face as he looked out the back window.

"Stop the bus!" he yelled.

His plead only ignited a group of hecklers. And then, true to his clumsy form, Seefer's foot landed in a pothole that sent him flying onto the asphalt. As he lay on the ground with scraped knees and pebbles stuck in his hand, and heard the uproar of laughter emanating from the departing bus.

Hector slid down the bus window and shouted, "Nice one, Seef!"

Seefer's blood reached a boiling point. He pounded the pavement. "Miffle!" He had never been one to handle his anger well, and this episode was no exception. Since he was very young, Seefer had always let frustrating situations get the best of him. He usually found a way to break, throw or physically beat something nearby. However, when faced with a challenge in front of kids he was supposed to be *cool* in front of, he would bottle up the rage.

He picked himself up, turned away from the bus and began to head back to the house. Even though he appeared to play it off, his heart raced underneath. He choked on embarrassment and fury, rethinking the whole situation. *Why did I let myself fall? Why didn't I wake up earlier?* But before his thoughts went too far, he heard a loud mechanical thud.

When he turned around, he saw the bus had broken

down. Steam poured out of its engine. Seefer smirked, thinking that justice had been served. Just as his moment was getting a little bit better, he saw his mom standing outside of the house with raised arms.

"What the heck, Seef? You missed it?"

"It wasn't my fault. The bus broke down."

"Well, whatever the case, I'm going to be late for my showing," she said annoyed. "Hop in the car."

The Elliots pulled up to Harrison Middle School and noticed all of the students filtering into the building with prevalent orange colors.

"So you decided against the T-shirt?" mom asked.

"Mom, that shirt is for like a nine-year-old. I don't even know why I still have it."

"I certainly don't have the heart to throw it away. You used to look so cute in it," she said fondly, resisting the urge to pinch his cheek.

"Ewww, Mom."

She softened. "Seefy, I know I get on your case sometimes, but I just want you to know that I want you to live up to your potential. You need to be more responsible."

Seefer, looking down and away, was impatiently waiting for her to finish her morning lesson. Even though she was icing it up, he could sense criticism coming.

She continued, "Do you understand how your

actions affect others? Because you stayed up late, and couldn't wake up on time, I'm going to be late for work."

"Can we just save this for later?" he suggested with an attitude.

Seeing that she was not going to get through to him at the moment, she conceded. "Fine. You have a nice morning, okay? Remember to hand in the note. I'll see you at 10."

"Can't wait." Seefer left the car and started to walk away.

"Love you!" she shouted out of the cracked car window.

Mortified, Seefer turned around with a look like *what are you doing?*

She signed with her hands, "I love you."

Some girls near Seefer giggled. He shrunk into his shirt and walked away. His mom drove away happily smiling to herself.

Seefer continued with his head down and walked as fast as he could into the school. *It's bad enough fitting in around here without my mom helping me look like a total tool.*

Cassy Smith sat on a bench outside the school. She was decked out in bracelets, a headband, even sneakers to go with the Spirit Day theme. Orange and grey donned her from head to toe. She was quite hard to miss, but Seefer was so determined to get inside, he blew right past her.

"Seefer! Hey!"

He was not in the mood to talk to anyone at the moment, but he felt that Cassy shouldn't bear the brunt of his bad mood. She was always good to him. Since getting acquainted at the beginning of the year, Cassy was the closest thing he had to a friend. Seefer didn't have many before middle school – none, really. He welcomed having somebody who didn't view him as a complete outcast, even if that person wouldn't be his first choice as a friend.

Cassy was a bit dorky. She acted overzealously in response to things that were mundane to most people. Seefer remembered how excited she was when he lent her a scented colored pencil. She acted like she never saw one before. She laughed herself into stitches about its impracticality.

When they arrived at Harrison together, it seemed like a perfect fit. Seefer felt like he wouldn't be able to shake his role as *the freak*, the caricature that followed him throughout elementary school. Here was a girl in Cassy who could care less. He surely couldn't let her go, but always wondered why it was him she seemed to latch onto in the first place.

"Hey, Cass. Nice outfit."

"Oh this? Just something I threw together," she said gleefully.

"Really? You had all of this stuff lying around your house?"

"Well, since I went shopping for it on Saturday, sure," she said. "I am so psychoed about Spirit Day! It is fun already. Look at everybody."

"Psyched," Seefer corrected. That was another thing Seefer liked about Cassy. She comically blurted out the oddest words now and then as if she didn't fully grasp the English language.

The two entered the school.

"Where's your orange, Seef?" she asked.

"I'll put it on in a moment. I have to drop something off in the principal's office."

"Okay. I'll see you."

Seefer walked into the principal's office with his dismissal note in hand. No one was at the secretary's desk. While he waited, he pulled his orange button-down shirt out of his bag and put it on.

The encouraging posters on the wall provided some amusement during Seefer's wait. One showed a bunch of kids laughing while reading a book. The poster read, "Reading is Fun!" Seefer rolled his eyes. "Okay. Guess I better *read* then," he said with a laugh.

Another poster showed a weightlifter drinking a glass of milk. It read, "MILK: Be Mighty!" Seefer scoffed at it. He had drunk milk his entire life, but did not and probably would not ever look like that guy.

Tired of waiting, he left the note on the secretary's desk. As he turned to leave, a voice called out. "Don't leave it there, son. Come in, come in." Principal Witik had popped his head outside his office and motioned Seefer to enter.

Principal Witik was a decent man, a portly fellow who bumbled around the hallways looking to have a good conversation with any student who would listen. Children usually redirected their paths to avoid a talk with Witik. Everyone had heard his stories, yet he would repeat them as if he was telling them for the first time.

Seefer knew what was coming, but it was too late. He was caught in the current and had to accept his fate. "Yes, Principal Witik?"

"Mr. Elliot, come in here for a moment. What seems to be the trouble?"

"No trouble, sir. I have to drop off a note. I'm leaving for a doctor's appointment today."

Reading the note, Witik said with disappointment, "Today of all days? Such a shame!"

"Hopefully I'm back in time for the assembly," said Seefer.

"Still with the headaches?"

Seefer was surprised Principal Witik remembered some of his headache spells from the last few months. Mr. Witik always seemed so scatterbrained, but Seefer supposed that his frequent visits to the nurse's station next door were probably enough for him to be familiar with the situation.

"No, a checkup…I think…I don't know. My mom's

in charge of that stuff."

"Ah, yes, well I know how it is. When I was a boy…"

Oh boy! Seefer sensed the beginning of a long Principal Witik story. Then a small miracle occurred – a knock at the door!

"Can I help you?" Principal Witik asked.

A man entered the room dressed in navy blue from head to toe. His uniform was soiled and stained, completely unpresentable. He held a folded pair of work gloves in his hand that he twisted nervously. His face looked as worn as his clothes, both were greasy and battered. "I am Pavo. Here about the…"

"The new custodian, of course!" Principal Witik interrupted. "I nearly forgot!" He summoned him into the room.

He turned to Seefer, "I'm sorry to cut you short. Thank you, son."

Sorry? Seefer couldn't be happier with the excuse to leave the office.

"No trouble, sir." Seefer got up to leave, but Pavo made it difficult to get through the door. He stood there, stone-faced, barely acknowledging Seefer's attempt to leave.

"Excuse me, sir."

Pavo was in another place at that moment. He snapped out of his daze and let Seefer pass, but gave him a once over as he walked away.

Seefer overheard Principal Witik say as he left the office. "Pavo, my dear man, have a seat."

When Seefer left the office, he bumped into Cassy, who was still waiting for him in the hallway. "What took you so long?" she asked. "Why is your shirt stained?"

"It's nothing. Principal Witik got a hold of me."

"Oh boy. His talks can be murderers," she said.

"Killers," Seefer corrected as they began walking to homeroom.

"Oh right. Luckily that guy came in. What did you have to do in there anyway?"

"I'm leaving for a few hours today," he said sadly.

"You're going to miss Korvus the Magnificent?"

The thought of missing the assembly ate at Seefer. From what he'd heard, Korvus the Magnificent was one of the greatest acts in the entire state. He dazzles the crowd with hypnosis tricks, lasers, and science experiments that cause explosions.

"My mom thinks I'll be back before it starts," he said.

They arrived at class. The room was about three quarters full at the moment and their teacher, Mrs. Cody, shuffled through stacks of paper. She was a younger woman who had kids of her own. Seefer liked her because she often called in for a substitute due to scheduling problems with her babysitter. She was also a decent teacher and kind of nice, too.

Seefer sat down at his desk in the row nearest the window. Cassy veered off to her place three spots behind him.

As they settled in, the students from Bus 31 filtered into the classroom. A couple of girls looked annoyed, while some of the boys were excited by the morning's events. Hector was the last one to enter. His desk was one over and one back from Seefer's. Naturally, this seat arrangement was the source of great anxiety to Seefer, who always felt like he was being watched.

Seefer's neighbor, Jona Miller, asked Hector, "Where've you been, Hec?"

Hector, with a suspicious look at Seefer, answered, "Bus broke down."

"What are you looking at me for?" Seefer asked.

"Because things always seem to go wrong around you, Seef," Hector speculated. "I saw you run for the bus, take a huge digger, and the next thing I know we're all stuck on the side of the road."

Hector's suspicion wasn't too far off. A pattern of trouble seemed to follow Seefer since they met. During the first week of school, Hector and his cronies cornered Seefer in a bathroom. His outwardly wimpy appearance and tendency to be a loner made him an easy choice to bully. When they had him surrounded and cowering, the automatic flushers on the urinals activated and sprayed the boys, drawing any attention away from Seefer. Even though the geyser of disgusting toilet water surprised Seefer also, he was cunning enough to slip out during the distraction.

Ever since that event, Hector has had his suspicions about him. He couldn't put his finger on what exactly he didn't like about him, but he simply hated anyone different than him. And Seefer was his antithesis.

"Oh yeah, Hector, I broke the bus and made you wait in the cold," Seefer retorted with thick sarcasm. There were far worse things he'd like to do to Hector.

"Look, weirdo, just remember I'm always watching you," Hector threatened.

Seefer, without a witty comeback, made a doofy face that mocked Hector's mannerisms.

"That's enough, boys," Mrs. Cody said. Hector sat at his desk and Seefer stopped with the faces.

Mrs. Cody continued, "I know all of you are excited about the festivities today. In order to participate, we are going to have to be diligent in getting our work done this morning. Let's all get our science books out now so we can begin immediately after the pledge."

Taking the queue from their teacher, the students plugged their ears. The lousy PA system crackled and squealed before every morning session when Principal Witik's voice boomed over the loudspeaker.

"Students of Harrison, good morning. Let us all rise for the Pledge of Allegiance. 'I pledge allegiance...'"

Seefer seldom followed along with the Pledge. He found it more interesting to watch and time the raising of the flag. He would watch the selected person come

16

out of the school and cross the white stone fringe of the flagstaff. That's when the timing started. Then he'd stop once they left the area. The best time he'd seen this year was eight seconds.

Apparently, the new custodian, Pavo, had the honors this morning. He walked out to the flagpole, and crossed into the garden beneath it. He unfolded the flag, secured it to the rope's clips, and raised it up the pole. He did pretty well for a newbie. Seefer was impressed, but he did notice something odd. Pavo had hung the flag upside down.

Does he not notice? Pavo looked at it as he anchored the rope. Apparently not, since he ignored it and walked back into the school. What a flub for a first day flag-raiser, Seefer thought. However, he did it in nine seconds. Not bad for his first time out.

"…and justice for all."

The class finished the pledge of allegiance and sat down. Mrs. Cody didn't miss a beat. "Okay, class. Page 78. We left off on Friday talking about differences between plant cells and animal cells. Can anybody give me a quick recap?"

Typical of the first class on Monday, only one student raised her hand. That one hand belonged to Sally Thompson, an enthusiastic girl at the front of the class who always strained herself trying to get chosen for answers.

"Okay, Sally," said Mrs. Cody.

Sally started, "Well…plant cells have a hard

exterior known as a cell wall. The cell wall…"

WOOM WOOM WOOM WOOM!

The classroom lights flickered followed by a pounding bass sound from the school PA system. The students in the room turned and stared at the room's PA speaker with curious faces. Then everything stopped. The lights remained on. The bass noise disappeared.

"What the…?" Hector asked.

"Watch your language, Mr. Ramirez," Mrs. Cody reminded Hector. "But to answer your question, I have no clue."

The students remained paused waiting for something else to happen. When nothing more occurred, Mrs. Cody went back to business. "Okay, kids. Let's cont–"

Suddenly a high-pitched sound blasted through the room. Everyone plugged their ears to avoid the ringing. The noise wasn't exactly painful, but much like brakes on a train, it was loud and annoying.

That second noise ended quickly, and the students settled down, but it was only the start of more excitement in the class.

Cassy shouted out, "Mrs. Cody, I think something is wrong with Seefer!"

2

Mrs. Cody rushed over to Seefer, who clenched his head and rocked back and forth. She pushed some students away to provide some space.

"Seefer. Seefer, are you okay? Can you speak?"

Seefer, who had experienced headaches like this before, learned to cope with them. "Yes," he grunted.

He then took a deep breath and tried to calm himself. He slowly took his hands away from his head and looked up. Everyone in the room stared at him with freaked-out faces.

"Something wrong?" he quipped.

"What happened to you?" Mrs. Cody asked.

"I don't even know," Seefer responded. "Guess that noise set me off."

"What a freak!" Hector added.

Mrs. Cody shot him a look as to say *sit down and shut up*. She tried to regain control of the chaos. "Okay, class. Take your seats or you're missing the show later." The students took no chances and quietly fell in line. She then turned to Seefer, "Are you really okay?"

"Yeah. It's happened a bunch of times. I'm fine." Seefer tried to be as cool as possible since this was the first time he had one of these spells in front of so many people.

"Well needless to say, you have to go to the nurse's station immediately," she insisted.

"I really don't need to," he assured her.

"No debating it. Jona, walk him down."

Jona shrugged. "Awww. Not me."

Hector whispered, "C'mon, Jona. Got to take care of your bestest friend." Jona shot back a sneer.

Mrs. Cody snapped. "Boys! Kids! Enough!"

"I can take him," Cassy offered from the back.

"I need someone a little bit bigger, Cassy. Someone he can lean on if he has to," she said. Cassy didn't like being told she couldn't handle it. "Jona, escort Seefer down to the office at once. End of story."

Jona reluctantly rose from his seat and held out his hand to give Seefer a boost out of his chair. Seefer proceeded slowly and staggered to the door.

The secretary was now at her desk in the main office. Mrs. Karcher was an older, plump woman who enjoyed her job at the school. She prided herself as being the grandmotherly figure in the school community. When she saw Seefer walk through the door, she immediately came over to care for him.

"You poor thing! Sit. Sit," she insisted. "What

happened to you?"

"Not feeling well," he responded.

Jona piped in, "Do I need to stay here?"

"No, you can go," Mrs. Karcher said.

Jona muttered, "Thank you, heavens" as he pumped his fist while leaving the office.

Mrs. Karcher directed Seefer to a seat near her desk. "You sit right here and relax, dear. I'll get Nurse Wendy here on the double."

Mrs. Karcher walked over to the PA system and tried to make an announcement, but it didn't work. "Such strange things happening this morning. She's down the hall. Will you be okay sitting here, if I go fetch her?"

"Yeah, I'll be fine," said Seefer.

"Okay, I will be right back."

Left to wait, Seefer stared out the office window. From his vantage point, he could see down the main corridor of the building. He would have loved to watch people bustling in the halls, but everyone was in class at the moment. Then he focused in on a conversation he could hear behind the principal's door.

Even though the slightly askew door dampened the sound, he could make out the words. Principal Witik was talking to someone on the phone: "I'm letting you know in case this messes up anything on your end. We have some people looking into the problem, but if you require any type of power source, it may not be here for you…oh…I see. Well, that's fantastic. Boy, the children are going to be so happy. I remember when I was a child, I always looked forward to…I'm sorry?…Oh, okay, we'll see you later."

He hung up the phone and called out to the main office for Mrs. Karcher. "Judy, it looks like the entertainment won't be affected. They can do their thing in the dark for all they care. I hope that new janitor figures out what the heck happened this morning."

Seefer was the only other person in the office. "Uh, Principal Witik? Mrs. Karcher isn't out here."

Witik came out of his office. "Mr. Elliot? You're back again?"

"Another headache," Seefer responded.

"Good thing you came in with that note today, then, eh?" Witik said with little compassion. "I'm sure Nurse Wendy will take fine care of you."

"Yes, sir."

"Now if you would excuse me, I've got to figure out what that darn noise was."

"I hope you find it." Seefer said. He found it odd that Principal Witik simply returned to his office after he'd said he needed to figure out the problem. *That was the shortest conversation that man has ever had. He must be concerned.*

While Seefer continued to wait, he looked down the hallway. From the main office, he could see all the way to the far stairwell. Watching an empty corridor was so dull. *Where is that Nurse Wendy?*

A figure walked into frame at the far end of the hall. Seefer felt relieved there was now something to look at. *Who was it? What is he or she doing?* It was definitely an adult judging by the size. The person held something flashy in his or her hand. Seefer was frustrated that he didn't have a clear view. The glass window between him and the corridor contained security wire which obstructed his view.

The person appeared to be waving the glowing object up and down the walls, slowly scanning the lockers in front of each classroom. *Why?* With piqued interest, Seefer moved closer to the window. He could now see that the figure was definitely a man – or possibly Mrs. Coppertini, the lunch lady. Whoever it was, they were behaving oddly.

As he watched, Seefer kept asking himself what the object could be. *Is it his smart phone? Is he looking for something? What could be so interesting in this school? Should I tell someone?*

Now the man was close enough to see his identity – Pavo. The new custodian, who apparently had no manners and no idea how to raise a flag, continued his pattern of odd behavior. *Where did this guy come from?*

Pavo passed by four classrooms and his motion never changed. Up and down, he moved his glowing object along each wall. When he got to Seefer's homeroom, his device flashed. Pavo stopped and stood still facing the room. He held the object outwards toward the door and started tapping on it, like he was inputting numbers on a calculator. The device grew brighter.

"Mr. Elliot!" a voice startled him. Nurse Wendy entered the office with Mrs. Karcher. "You shouldn't be standing up. Mrs. Karcher told me what happened. You need to sit and relax."

"Sorry, Nurse Wendy."

Seefer looked out the window and saw lights swirling around the device in Pavo's hand. He wondered if he should point this out to the adults in the room.

"Seefer, I can take you in my office right away. Let me pull your file." She followed Mrs. Karcher behind the administrative area of the office.

Nurse Wendy was a kind woman with dark hair and skin. Even though she was in her mid-30s, she had worry lines on her face that made her look a little older than she really was. She looked through a tan filing cabinet for Seefer's medical folder. His was easy to find considering it was twice the size of anyone else's in that same drawer.

"Okay, I've got it. Come with me, Seefer."

"Wait." Seefer felt the need to point out the oddity in the hall. "Look at the new janitor. He's doing weird things in the hallway."

The nurse and secretary, slightly concerned by Seefer's phrasing, peered through the glass window into the hallway.

"Seefer, I'll have Principal Witik have a word with him. No one should be using their cell phones on school grounds while class is in session. Even the janitor," said Mrs. Karcher.

"Cell phone?" Seefer asked. He looked again at Pavo. The suspicious device was no longer glowing, flashing or surrounded by swirling lights. It actually did look like a cell phone, and Pavo appeared to be texting on it. "But you should have seen what it was…" He stopped. He realized the description would have been too ludicrous for anyone to believe.

"Seen what, Seefer?" Nurse Wendy asked.

"Never mind." With that, Seefer followed Nurse Wendy into her office to be examined.

In the nurse's station, sitting on the exam table, Nurse Wendy shined a light into Seefer's eyes. "Open," she said pointing to his mouth. She placed a wooden depressor on his tongue. "Say, 'ahhh.'"

"Ahhh."

She looked down his throat briefly and then shut off her exam light. "Okay. You don't look broken. How do you feel?"

"I feel fine now," he said.

"Tell me about what happened."

"We were in homeroom. We said the pledge. Then the lights started blinking, and that noise came on. All of sudden, my head was pounding."

Nurse Wendy gave Seefer a concerned look. "Then we better proceed with caution." She walked over to her desk and started writing a note. "You're going to your regular doctor today, I understand?"

"Yeah." Seefer acknowledged her, but he wasn't exactly giving his full attention. He couldn't stop thinking about what the custodian could be doing. *Where is he now? What was he looking for?*

"Seefer!" Nurse Wendy shouted to grab his attention. She handed him two notes. "This is for your doctor. Bring it to your appointment this morning. I wrote down what we discussed here." She handed him the second note. "This is for Mrs. Cody. No more physical activities for the rest of the day."

Yeah, right! Gym class followed first period, and he wasn't going to sit out while everyone else got to run wild. He was in middle school after all. Gym class was the last remnant of recess he had. So he kindly agreed to Nurse Wendy's request but had every intention to pocket the note. "Okay, Nurse Wendy."

"I'm going to try to get a hold of your mom now and let her know what's happened. Do you want to wait here, or go back to class?"

Without hesitation Seefer responded, "Class."

Nurse Wendy escorted Seefer into the main office area where Principal Witik reviewed some papers with Mrs. Karcher. As Nurse Wendy headed over to the secretary's desk, she reminded him, "Remember, no more activities!"

Right before he started out the door, Pavo entered. Seefer froze. *Does he know I was watching him?*

"Pavo! Where have you been?" Principal Witik inquired.

"I have been looking for breaks in the PA system, sir," Pavo responded.

Seefer felt silly for thinking there was something more to the sight he saw earlier. It made total sense to him now.

Witik called Pavo into the office, and Seefer continued to walk past him. He noticed the strange device hanging off of his tool belt. *So that's the device? Doesn't really look like a smart phone up close.* As they passed each other, Seefer's curiosity carried him too close and he bumped into Pavo. The device came to life. A whirring noise emanated from it and lights began to flicker.

Oh no! Did I break it? Seefer didn't know what it meant, but he didn't want to find out. He put his head down and kept walking. Maybe if he walked quickly enough, the device would turn off, and the whole thing would go unnoticed.

In the hallway, Seefer picked up the pace. He got about two classrooms away, when he couldn't take the curiosity any longer. He had to turn around. When he did, he made direct eye contact with Pavo, who had been watching him the whole way.

3

Seefer put on his school-issued sweats in the boys' locker room. Most of the other boys finished and waited around for the Phys. Ed. teacher to call them out to gym class.

As Seefer tried to stuff his foot through a balled up pant leg, an audience built around him, snickering. Feeling the pressure of a dozen eyes on him, he started to freak out that his wardrobe change wasn't going smoothly enough. Frustrated, he jabbed his foot several times to break through the ball instead of perhaps the easier route, unraveling it with his fingers.

"Hey guys, look," Hector said in a mocking tone. "I'm Seefer, and I need to get inside my locker." He began grunting like an ape while he pounded the door and rattled the handle.

One of Hector's cronies, Donny, aided the visual. "No, Seefer, this is how you do it." He opened the locker by pulling up on the lever. Hector, still imitating an ape, scratched his head and grunted in confusion.

All the other boys roared with laughter. Seefer stared blankly at them before finishing up with his sneakers.

Without a word, Seefer rose up and walked through the boys toward the locker room exit.

Hector shouted, "Oh come on, Seefer. No sense of humor?"

Seefer turned around, began scratching his head and armpits, and said "Oo oo ah ah. Me no understand." Then he turned the corner to leave.

A few of the boys burst out laughing, but clammed up their smiles when Hector sneered at them.

Seefer's entire class gathered on the baseball diamond outside the school. The morning chill had left the air to make for a pleasant autumn day.

Cassy found Seefer amongst the group of people and gave him a nudge. "Are you feeling alright?"

"Just dandy," he replied.

Coach Wilhelm stomped out onto the field with a red kickball in hand. The class bunched into a circle around the pitcher's mound.

"Okay, class, listen up! Let's get started quickly so we waste no time in having fun. We're playing kickball today." The class cheered. "I need two captains right now."

Coach chose Hector and the ever-eager Sally as captains. They immediately started choosing their sides.

Sally went first, "Lance."

Then Hector, "Jonas."

Then Sally again, "Olivia."

And Hector, "Donny."

They traded back and forth, separating into their two teams. Cassy and Seefer stood in the middle of the unpicked kids watching one after another being plucked before them.

"This is all so familiar," Cassy said as she looked at the other six in the group. Seefer nodded in agreement.

Sally shouted, "Cassy!"

"Oh my! They picked *me*!" Cassy ran out to Sally's group happily.

The next three students are picked. As usual, this left Seefer and Freda Rijul, a highly frail and introverted girl who donned headgear and a leg brace. Logically, she should be anyone's last pick, but since Hector was picking next...

"Freda," he said. Shocked, Freda limped over to his team.

"Okay, Elliot, you're on Sally's team," interjected Coach. "Let's get this started."

The students huddled up with their teams and gave themselves pep talks. Sally's team took the field as Hector's team prepared to come to the plate.

Without direction, Seefer took right field, where he's always sent anyway. He noticed how happy Cassy was to take second base, thirty feet in front of him.

When she ran out to her position, she gave a very enthusiastic thumb's up to Seefer in the outfield.

Team Hector's first batter was Jona. Everyone knew he was speedy on the bases. Team Sally adjusted their positions to prepare for a possible bunt. After the fielders shifted, Hector shouted, "Jona. Right field!"

Jona looked out to right and saw Seefer barely paying attention. He stared up at some passing clouds. Jona turned back to Hector with a nod and a smile.

When Sally rolled the first pitched of the game, Jona charged and creamed the ball over Cassy and into the outfield. She turned and saw Seefer not watching. "Seefer! Head up! Head up!"

Seefer snapped out of his daze and scrambled to get under the ball. "I got it! I got it!" He shuffled back a few steps and planted himself where he thought the ball would come down. When the ball was about to land, he readjusted and fell backwards. The ball smacked him square in the chest, and bounced ten feet back in the air.

"Get it in!" Cassy shouted.

"C'mon, hurry!" another teammate yelled.

He rushed over to the ball, picked it up and tossed it in. By the time it rolled into the infield, Jona had rounded all the bases and scored. Hector's team celebrated the run.

Dejected, Seefer walked back to his position. He could hear the third basemen talking to the shortstop. "Why do we even have to play him in the field? This happens all the time!" he said.

Seefer tried his best to shake the comment off. *Not again. It's not going to happen again.*

While Seefer tried to psyche himself into the game, the other players focused on the next batter, Davis. With all of attention at home plate, no one noticed a little visitor entering the field. A sickly looking rat wandered behind the left fielder. It had a patchy coat of wiry hair and cloudy eyes that looked filled with milk. The rodent sniffed around looking for something.

Sally rolled the ball. Everyone's eyes were glued to the kicker. No one noticed that three more rats came onto the field.

Davis charged the ball and hit a long, high shot into right field. Everyone gazed as the ball sailed over the infield. As the ball peaked and began its descent, someone discovered the invading vermin.

"Rats!" shouted Sally.

Seefer yelled out, "No! I got this!" He shuffled around trying to get under the ball, ignoring the screams coming from the infield.

Coach Wilhelm yelled out to everybody, "Kids! Off! Now!"

Dozens more rats poured out onto the field. They crawled up to students' feet sniffing them out as they ran for their dear lives.

Seefer, clueless to the on goings, looked up. The kickball followed a direct path to his position. He opened up his arms and hoped for the best. Miraculously, it fell right into his grasp.

"I got it? I got it! Wahoo!" Seefer looked around for adulation, but everyone was fleeing. *What the heck is going on?*

Seefer turned to his right and saw the other two outfielders running for the break in the fence by the scoreboard. They didn't make it before two rats leapt onto each of their backs. The kids flailed their arms trying to get them off, but it was no use. The rats climbed up their shirts onto their heads. The rodents stuck their large snouts into the children's ears, sniffed for a moment and then scurried off.

Seefer froze. *Why was this happening?* There were rats everywhere. The third-baseman was four feet up the chain link fence in front of the dugout. A rat dangled off his pant leg, making its way toward his head.

Seefer looked at the bleachers. Most of Hector's team was up on the top row moving their feet like tap dancers. Coach Wilhelm stood two rows lower than them, swatting rats away with his whiteboard pad. Seefer would normally be amused at such a sight, but this scene overwhelmed him so much, he had no time to snicker.

"Git outta here, you garbage eatin' vermin!" Coach shouted as he sent one sailing into the fence.

Seefer looked back onto the field. Only one person remained – Cassy. He couldn't believe that she was the only one left, not running, but facing the rats head on. One rat leapt up onto her leg. She took it between her hands and snapped its neck. *Whoa!!!*

"Cassy!" Seefer shouted. *Did I just see what I think I saw?* He had always perceived Cassy not only as a girl, but an especially dorky girl who certainly didn't seem the type to ward off vermin. But there she was, fending off big, disgusting rats.

Some students ran far enough away from the field where the rats didn't bother pursuing them any further. Those rats returned.

"Don't let them near your face!" Cassy shouted out.

Seefer noticed that he caught one's attention. It stood before him and looked up at Seefer with its milky white eyes. Seefer didn't flee. He stood still as he had for the minutes since catching that ball.

The rat inched toward his foot. Seefer took a step back. The rat paused but then crawled toward him again. Seefer took the kickball in his hand and spiked it toward the creature. It took the hit but then turned back to him with an angry face. *Shouldn't have done that, Seef.*

The rat hissed and leapt up at him. Seefer tried to grab it like Cassy did, but missed it. He lost his balance and fell to the ground. The rat clawed up his shirt and burrowed its nose into Seefer's ear. After a sniff and a nuzzle, the rat freed itself.

It crawled up onto Seefer's chest and then squealed out. *Is it calling the others?* Seefer panicked and whacked it three feet away with the back of his hand.

But it was too late. Seefer watched as the other rats ceased their pursuit of the other kids. Even the one between Cassy's hands stopped attacking as it turned its attention to Seefer.

He was now very alarmed. Did he agitate matters more by swatting the squealer? Seefer quickly got to his feet and stared at over fifty rats closing in on him.

"Nice mousies," Seefer said. "You don't want a guy like me. Nobody ever chooses me."

He slowly backed away from them, but they continued their approach. Closer and closer they came. A sea of smelly, disgusting sewer dwellers surrounded Seefer, staring back at him. Each rat had its cloudy, vacant eyes fixed on his face.

Cassy saw Seefer in trouble and felt compelled to help, but first she had to get rid of the rat in her hands. She wound up, and chucked it over the backstop of the field, then quickly ran to his aide.

But as Cassy made her way to right field, the rats standing before Seefer squealed in unison. They raised each little snout in the air, hissing and squeaking. The sound grew until the rats suddenly sprung at Seefer. Again, he fell to the ground. They covered his entire body, giving the appearance of a dirty, wiry-haired blanket.

No longer pursued by rats of their own, the other students' attention turned to Seefer. Some came back onto the field to get a closer look, but no one dared to help, not even Coach Wilhelm. They stood silent and frightened.

"Hang on, Seefer!" Cassy sprung atop the pile and grabbed as many as she could, then hurled them over the fence. She had no fear of being clawed or bitten. Her only goal was to free Seefer.

She heard his voice from beneath the pile. He yelled for her. It sounded like, "I'm okay," but how could that be? She grew more determined to help.

"Seefer, hold on!" she shouted. Cassy was close to tears herself.

She tossed at least a dozen rats away from Seefer, though more were coming.

WOOM WOOM WOOM WOOM!

The noise returned – the same one from that morning's homeroom. Everyone paused. Even the rats seemed a little distracted.

It lasted only a few seconds. When it ended, the rats peeled away and scurried into the woods. Cassy shooed the last ones around Seefer's head, revealing his face again. He wasn't crying at all. He had been laughing the whole time.

"Seefer, you are alright? I thought you were suffering," she said.

"I said I was okay," he told her as he rose to his feet, sending the remaining rats away.

"How? You were covered."

"I know! They were so ticklish!" he said with a laugh.

Cassy punched him in the arm, probably hard enough to leave a bruise.

"Now, *that* hurt!" he said while rubbing his arm.

Seefer looked around and saw a tide of gawkers coming his way. He figured Hector and Jona were obviously going to ridicule him. Surprisingly, they were at a loss for words.

Coach Wilhelm came the closest to him, solely out of duty. He awkwardly patted Seefer on the back. "Good work, son."

Sally had a disgusted look on her face. "Ewww. You are covered in rat turds."

Coach flicked one off of Seefer's shoulder. The class erupted in laughter.

Seefer couldn't tell whether they were laughing at him or the Coach's gesture. Then he heard someone say, "You are what you're covered in."

Yup, they're definitely laughing at me.

Cassy gave him a consoling look. "Never mind them. Let's go." They started walking away.

Refusing to look back, Seefer and Cassy walked toward the break in the fence. As they headed in that direction, they noticed someone over in the opposite dugout – Pavo. He sat on the bench watching them cross the field. He had his strange device in-hand as well. *Had he been there this whole time?*

When Pavo saw Seefer and Cassy looking at him, he stood up from the bench and walked out of sight.

"Cassy, that guy over there is up to something."

"Should we tell coach?" she asked.

Seefer considered it for a moment. He turned back with the words on his tongue's tip, but saw the crowd of kids still laughing at his expense. Coach Wilhelm did nothing to stop it. "No, never mind."

4

Seefer and Cassy were alone inside Mrs. Cody's room. Seefer sat at his desk with his head in his hands, while Cassy perched herself beside him on the window sill. They left Coach Wilhelm's class early though they weren't granted permission to do so. Getting in trouble was the least of their worries, however.

"So how exactly would a school janitor be able to do that?" Cassy asked.

"I don't know. I've seen him four times this morning. Four! And it's only his first day. I don't ever remember seeing the last janitor, and he was here for like *years*."

"So?" she asked.

"So! Well, I haven't really figured out exactly how he's responsible, but I know for sure he doesn't like me. I think I may have bumped into one of his tools in the office this morning and I may have broken it. He gave me creepy looks the whole time I walked back to class," Seefer said.

"And that is how he summoned the supernatural ability to control animals that inevitably did you no harm?" Cassy asked with a smile.

Seefer then realized the ridiculousness of it all and began to shake his head in confusion. "Yes. Uh…wait…I don't know."

Cassy said, "Blaming the janitor is not going to explain the behavior of those rats. They nipped and scratched every other student out there, but you were not even hurt. You were covered with them."

"Do feelings count?" Seefer asked.

"No." she said wryly.

"Okay. Then I'm good."

The school bell rang, and the other kids returned to the classroom. The first few to enter gave very awkward looks toward Cassy and especially to Seefer.

Cassy added quietly, "We will figure it out. Do not jump to conclusions so eagerly."

The next bunch of kids walked in, led by Hector.

"Hey, it's Rat Boy!" Hector exclaimed, followed by an imitation of a mouse nibbling cheese.

Jona came in right behind him chanting, "Rat boy! Rat boy!"

Even Victoria, a girl who hardly ever spoke, made a point to comment when she walked by Seefer's desk. "It was pretty gross when you were covered in all that poop."

"Thank you for letting me know. I'm clean *now*!"

"Then what's that on your shirt?" she asked while pointing.

He looked down and saw the spot his mom noticed earlier. "That? You know, I wasn't wearing this shirt outside. It's a food stain."

"More like a poo stain," Hector interjected.

The class erupted in laughter at Seefer's expense. Exasperated, he put his head down on the desk. People were too busy pointing and laughing to notice that some of the classroom computers were flickering.

Cassy erupted at Hector, "Why are you always above everyone, Hector? You were not so *cold* on the baseball seats! You squeaked louder than a snard in a rain storm!"

Hector looked stunned. Cassy never spoke a word to him before, but she just threw some fierce, yet somewhat confusing, words his way. "What the heck are you talking about?" he retorted.

"You got burned!" Jona heckled. "I think."

Seefer picked his head up, "Yes, he did. That was a burn."

"Whatever, Seefer! You going to let a girl do all of your talking?" Hector asked.

"If I don't have much to say, sure, why not?" Seefer responded with an honest tone.

"And is she going to come to your rescue when your freak self is covered in mice?"

"Maybe. What's the big deal?" Seefer asked.

"Because…" Hector paused. Seefer was actually pretty good about countering Hector's verbal assaults with reason. He figured there wasn't anything to lose by answering him with anything other than honest replies. Hector grew more flustered with each passing second and resorted to a witless attack. "Because, you're a freak, Seefer. A stupid rat freak!"

Seefer smiled as Hector unraveled. "I was just asking," he said.

"Whoa! Check it out!" another student yelled pointing out the window. Everyone rushed over to take a look.

A large box truck pulled into the front parking lot of the school. It looked like a converted delivery vehicle with antennas mounted on the top. The side had a mural of atoms, math formulas and the solar system. Giant letters spelled, "KORVUS THE MAGNIFICENT'S SCIENCE-MOBILE."

"He's here!" Davis said with child-like glee.

The truck drove up to the front of the school and stopped in the fire lane. The passenger side door opened and a mysterious figure emerged. He donned a silver cloak which had a hood that covered his head.

All of the kids in Mrs. Cody's room waited to see more. They eagerly pressed their heads against the window. Cassy, the only one who didn't have the child-like wonder in her eyes, looked on with suspicion.

Michael, a somewhat rambunctious child, couldn't take waiting anymore. He cracked the window and yelled, "Hey Korvus the Magnificent!" Then he waved excitedly.

The cloaked man turned upward and observed with his beady yellow eyes. His entrance attracted an audience of onlookers. He removed his hood, revealing his zebra streaked hair and eccentric beard. *So that's Korvus!* He gestured to the class as to say *thank you.* His attention then turned to the main entrance, as Principal Witik came out to greet him.

"Class!" shouted Mrs. Cody while entering the room. "Take your seats."

The kids jumped away from the window and found their desks. They settled quickly and opened their math books.

After all of the excitement that had happened that morning, math class completely dragged. Mrs. Cody reviewed some of the standard units of length and drew no interest from the students. She needed to engage them better, so she picked up a whiteboard eraser.

"Can anyone tell me what would be the best unit of measure to determine the length of this eraser?" she asked. To her surprise, Cassy raised her hand. She seldom volunteered, so Mrs. Cody happily pointed to her for the answer.

Cassy replied, "Centimeters."

Mrs. Cody looked at the eraser and gauged it. "Yes, perhaps. Let's stay away from the metric system for a moment. Anyone else?"

Sally raised her hand eagerly, and then spoke before being chosen. "Inches, Mrs. Cody."

"Correct. This eraser is about four inches long. It is much more proper than say, feet or yards."

From the back of the class, Cassy started to snicker.

"Something funny, Cassy?" Mrs. Cody asked.

Almost unable to contain laughter, Cassy struggled to get out a sentence. "Inches are so antiquated! I forgot that they are still used here!"

Seefer turned to Cassy and mouthed the word, "antiquated" with a puzzled face.

Also confused, Mrs. Cody asked, "*Here?*"

Cassy's eyes bulged for a moment. Then she answered definitively. "America. I spent some time in Europe. I got very used to those dang centimeters."

The class chuckled.

"Well, Cassy is correct in that most of the world uses the metric system," Mrs. Cody said. "But the imperial system – inches, feet, miles – has its uses as well."

Cassy started to laugh again.

"Okay, Cassy. That's enough." Cassy's laughter stirred some whispering with other students.

Cassy pushed her luck. "Say, exactly how many feet are in one mile?"

Mrs. Cody sighed. "I'm not sure, Cassy. Why don't you tell the class?"

"I do not know, either," Cassy said. "It is some

ridiculous number, but do you know how many centimeters are in one kilometer? 100,000! How simple is that?!"

"You made your point."

But Cassy continued. "And you know how many centiliters are in a liter? One hundred. Ounces in a gallon? Thirty-two? Sixty-four? Who knows?"

"This is your last warning, young lady." Mrs. Cody's tone turned serious. Cassy was not only challenging the system, but taking her teacher down with it. Students in the class stared intently with wide eyes, like witnesses to a train wreck.

Cassy, with a smirk on her face, breathed deep and asked, "And what is the deal with Fahrenheit?"

"That's it!" Mrs. Cody slammed her book down. "You are going to the office right now!"

Cassy stood up and walked to the front of the class. Along the way, Seefer made eye contact with her and whispered, "What's gotten into you?" Cassy ignored him.

When she walked past Mrs. Cody, she received some words from her. "I don't know where this acting up is coming from, but you need to rethink your current behavior."

Cassy turned before leaving the room. "Yes, Mrs. Cody." Then she exited.

A dozen conversations erupted at the moment the door closed. Mrs. Cody quickly put an end to it. "Can we please get through this without any more distractions?" she asked the class. The class settled. The students squared up to the front of room and reset themselves.

"Now. Where were we?" Mrs. Cody asked.

But almost instantly, someone knocked on the classroom door. Mrs. Cody huffed in frustration as she answered. Pavo stepped into the room. Seefer immediately scrunched down in his chair. *What's he doing here? I'm dead.*

The two adults talked quietly at the door threshold. Seefer watched as Pavo scanned the room, looking over each desk. When his eyes landed on Seefer, he stopped scanning. *Uh-oh!*

Mrs. Cody turned and looked at Seefer too. *What did he say to Mrs. Cody?* She said a few more things to Pavo, but then turned and called, "Seefer, a moment?"

Quietly, Hector whispered to him, "Ooooo, someone's in trouble."

Seefer ignored him as he walked to the door. As he came closer to Pavo, his fears increased. *What is he going to do to me?*

"Seefer, please assist Mr. Pavo. He needs some help setting up for today's assembly," Mrs. Cody said.

Some students moaned because they assumed Seefer would be assisting the great Korvus. That thought never crossed Seefer's mind. He was sure this had everything to do with his and Pavo's second encounter. Seefer nodded to Mrs. Cody's request with uneasiness, and then followed Pavo out into the hallway.

As they began walking, Seefer already knew the excuse Pavo gave his teacher was untrue. They were heading away from the gymnasium, which was near the main entrance. *If the assembly is supposed to be in the gym, where are we going?*

Seefer could still see the main office, but didn't see any sign of Cassy waiting there. He wondered if she was swiftly brought into the principal's office for discipline.

Pavo spoke not a word while leading Seefer to the back of the building. To break the tension, Seefer decided to start some small talk. "The name's Seefer Elliot," he said with a forced enthusiasm.

"Greetings," Pavo said bluntly.

"Stud finder?" Seefer said looking at the device on Pavo's belt.

Pavo turned and covered the device with his hand. "Yes," he said shortly.

"Guess that's why I set it off earlier, huh?" Seefer said with a goofy grin.

Pavo didn't find that funny. "It is very expensive."

Seefer rolled his eyes. He thought he was surely in trouble. Adults never have a sense of humor when they're about to discipline a child.

The walk remained silent for the rest of the way. Pavo led Seefer into the basement of the school. He had never been down there before. There was never a reason to go. All classrooms and activity rooms were found on the first and second floor. The basement was a place for storage, utilities and the janitor's room.

The janitor's room! Seefer now feared he had seen the last of the surface world. He thought Pavo was going to make him a prisoner of some sort.

"We're here," Pavo said.

Seefer stood before the door of the workshop. The dimly lit threshold was less than inviting. The basement was dark and damp throughout, but the entrance to Pavo's room seemed more so.

Pavo opened the squeaky metal door and turned on the light. Seefer could see all the way back to the staircase which led outside. He debated making a run for it now.

He followed Pavo into the room. Power tools and garden equipment hung from hooks on the walls. Large boxes filled with cleaning supplies littered the floor. Seefer heard a very distinct noise coming from the back of the room – a noise he became very familiar with that morning.

"Are there rats in here?" Seefer asked.

Pavo clicked a light switch that brightened up the back of the room. When the shadows lifted, Seefer saw cages stacked in the corner of the workshop. There were at least ten, each stuffed with those gross cloudy-eyed rats from the baseball diamond. Seefer was curious, fearful, and confused all at the same time.

"Are these the rats I saw earlier?" he asked.

Pavo responded, "Yes."

He handed Seefer a piece of cheese and motioned him to feed them. When Seefer held the cheese out to the five rats in the top cage, they all scrambled to eat it. Each one grabbed a chunk.

Pavo continued, "The rats are not what you are here for. I need your help with something else. Come over here."

Before Seefer followed, he looked at the rats he fed. They were all lying motionless on the floor of the cage. *Did I feed them poison?*

"Mr. Pavo? The rats–"

"Not now! Come." Pavo instructed.

Despite feeling horribly guilty, Seefer silently obeyed. Pavo held out his hand for him to sit down at a table in the room. The old rickety table looked swelled and moldy from being in the basement for years. Seefer hesitated to sit down, but decided not to anger this guy in any way.

Pavo pulled out a shiny metal case he had hiding under a tarp. He dropped it on the table. It made a loud thud indicating how heavy the case must have been. The table didn't look built for heavy duty use. Seefer wondered how long it could handle the weight.

Pavo opened the case, revealing an array of gadgetry. All of them had the sleek silvery finish that his *stud finder* had. Cutouts in black foam gave each device its own place. There was an empty space that looked to be the same shape as the thing on Pavo's belt.

"Whoa, cool stuff," Seefer commented.

Pavo answered dryly, "standard tool set."

Seefer watched intently as Pavo managed the equipment in his case. He removed the device from his belt and stowed it in the empty cavity. Next, he removed a small cube attached to a glass chamber. He set this up on the table and entered a code. The cube produced a humming sound while a touch screen interface appeared. While it continued to hum, Pavo took out what looked like a basic pen. It was shiny metal, like everything else, but it didn't look electronic or exciting at all.

Pavo handed the pen to Seefer. He thought it was odd that there was such a basic tool in a box full of such elaborate equipment.

"What is this?" Seefer asked.

"Click it," said Pavo.

There was a small button on top of the device much like a click-pen. At this point Seefer assumed it *was* a pen. He clicked the button with his thumb.

An incredible pain shot through his thumb. "Monkey fudge!" Seefer yelled. His grip on the device loosened, and Pavo quickly reached in to grab it. As the pen came out, Seefer realized that something inside of the pen came out and stuck him. Blood squirted all over the top of the instrument and his finger.

Pavo placed the pen inside the glass tube attached to the cube. "Silly me. I forgot to put the child-lock on it. I am sorry." He tossed Seefer a gauze pad for his finger.

"Is there something strange about this gauze that I should know about?" Seefer asked.

"Unless you think stopping bleeding is strange, no," he responded.

Seefer put the pad on his finger as Pavo took out a pair of silver glasses from his case. He stared at the cube as it performed some activity. The lights on it shined brighter, and the noise hummed louder. Pavo looked up at Seefer and warned, "You might want to close your eyes."

Seefer closed them before a bright flash emanated from the cube. When the brightness faded, he hesitantly opened one eye. After everything appeared normal, he opened the other.

Pavo sat in the chair staring at the cube almost with a sense of accomplishment. He muttered the word, "Cepheus." Seefer noticed that the light had changed from blue to green on the box.

"Good sign?" he asked.

Pavo nodded. "Yes indeed."

"Cool. So I thought we were going to set up for the assembly or something. If you don't need me to help, I can leave now."

"No, that would not be wise. You need to stay with me," Pavo told him.

Seefer blurted out, "Creepy." Pavo shot him a look. Seefer retracted, "No offense. Sorry."

"Come. Follow me."

"Where?" Seefer asked.

Pavo paused to think then said, "We need to run a few errands."

Seefer followed Pavo back upstairs and into the main hallway. They were headed toward the school's main entrance. Seefer didn't know what errands Pavo had in store for him. *Are we going to the office? The gym? Leaving school altogether?* He had been left in the dark.

As they came within steps of the main office, Principal Witik popped out from one of the gymnasium doors.

"Mr. Pavo. How did you make out with the PA system?" he asked.

"It is working." Pavo replied.

"Excellent. Say, would you mind assisting the entertainment in setting up? There are a few things they have questions about."

Seefer wondered why Pavo was being asked now. *Wasn't he supposed to be doing that in the first place?*

"We will be right there." Pavo said.

From behind Principal Witik, the silvery cloaked Korvus emerged. He dropped his hood. When he caught sight of Pavo, an air of familiarity struck his face. Seefer sensed Pavo had a mutual recognition toward

Korvus. Before he could see anymore, Pavo used his hand to guide Seefer behind his body, obstructing his view.

"The stage lighting room is locked," Korvus said.

"I can open that." Pavo ensured. He held out his hand inviting Korvus to re-enter the gym. Once he left, Pavo quickly turned to Seefer.

"Go. Do not come back here." Pavo whispered.

"Go where?" Seefer asked.

But Principal Witik prevented any further conversation. He interrupted, "Now, Pavo. Go help the entertainment. We need this show to go on."

So Pavo nodded in agreement and entered the gym.

Principal Witik returned to his office.

Seefer stood confused at the nexus of the office, gym, hallway and the exit. *Where am I supposed to go again?*

"Seefer?" said a familiar voice from outside.

He turned around and saw his mother standing at the entrance.

"Mom?"

"Is that the shirt I told you not to wear today?" she asked.

Seefer was lost for an answer.

"Are you ready for your appointment?" she asked through gritted teeth.

Suddenly, Seefer wished he were back in math class.

5

Seefer's pupil shrank from a large dose of bright light. Doctor Brees held her ophthalmoscope an inch away from his eye, looking into it for anything peculiar.

"Looks good in there," said the doctor. "Why don't you tell me what's been going on?"

Dr. Brees put her instrument away and rolled her stool up to Seefer and his mom.

"We saw you a few months back after Seefer was experiencing a series of headaches," his mom explained. "The medicine you prescribed helped for a while, but they slowly came back. Within the last month, they've become more frequent."

The doctor asked, "How frequent?"

His mom paused a moment to think. "Every other day or so."

"More," Seefer said.

"More?" the doctor asked. "When was the last time you had one?'

"Today. At the beginning of school."

"Honey! Why didn't you tell me?" his mom asked.

"It didn't seem that important. It was over quick."

"Seefy, everything that happens to you is important. Don't be afraid to tell me."

"Well, I knew we were going to be coming here anyway. I was feeling fine by the time I saw the nurse." He then remembered the note Nurse Wendy gave him. "Oh! She gave me this to give to you, doc."

Seefer handed the doctor the note. She read it quietly but made noises of interest along the way. When finished, she paused to think for a moment while thumbing through his medical records.

"Seefer, have you had any epileptic episodes?"

Seefer looked at her strangely. He was stuck on the word *epileptic*.

"Seizures, honey?" his mom asked.

"No."

"Do you ever lose consciousness whenever you get one of your headaches?" Dr. Brees asked.

"No. I remember the whole thing," replied Seefer.

"How do you feel after?" the doctor said while taking careful notes.

"Fine," he said with a shrug.

"How about outside of the headaches? Do you experience dizziness or nausea?"

"Nausea is like sea-sickness, right?" he asked. Dr. Brees nodded back. "I don't think so."

"Numbness in the hands or feet? Twitches? Odd

smells or visions? Heart-racing?" Dr. Brees went on to ask a list of symptoms, but Seefer didn't identify with any of them.

"How about drooling?"

Seefer laughed. "No!"

"Interesting. Your nurse pointed out some strange occurrences at the school that could have triggered your episode this morning. Epileptics commonly respond negatively to things like noise or flashing lights. And other things like stress, lack of sleep, or too much caffeine can compound the issue."

Seefer looked mortified. *Am I the cause of my own problems?* His mother constantly told him to get a good night sleep and not drink so much soda. "I think I had a dose of all of those this morning."

"Are you saying my son has epilepsy?" mom asked.

"Not necessarily. Besides the headaches, he doesn't have any other red flag symptoms. Hard to say without running further tests. I can refer you to a great neurologist who would conduct some scans to see what's going on up there." She pointed to Seefer's head.

The doctor added, "The good news is that he comes away every time feeling fine, looking fine. If we can figure out what is triggering the headaches, then we'll be able to take away all of the discomfort."

Mom asked "Why recently and not ever before? This has been going on for less than six months."

"He's twelve, right?" checked the doctor.

"Yes," Seefer and his mom answered concurrently.

The doctor asked. "Seefer, is your body going through any other changes?"

"Like what?" Seefer asked with a furrowed brow.

"Oh, you know. Around your age, some boys' voices get deeper. They sweat more and might need to use deodorant. You might get hair in places you didn't have before."

Seefer and his mom squirmed uncomfortably in their seats. Dr. Brees recognized this, but continued.

"Puberty," she said. "Sometimes changes in one part of the body can cause changes, both positive and negative, in other parts."

"Uggh," his mother said. "I think I'm getting a headache of my own."

6

After the humiliating and awkward conversation that transpired at the doctor's office, Seefer's mom tried to make things better by treating him to a meal at his favorite burger joint, Wabba Burger. Sitting before a giant double cheeseburger and curly fries, he couldn't stop thinking about the possibility of missing the fun at school.

"What's bothering you, kiddo?" asked his mom.

"Nothing." He dipped some fries in ketchup before devouring the handful. He stared off into the distance as he chewed.

"Do you want to talk about anything?"

Seefer shook his head.

"Why didn't you tell me about your episode this morning?" she asked.

"I don't know. The nurse said she was going to call you."

"I was with a client," Mom regretfully admitted. "I'm sorry I didn't check for the message."

"Well, it didn't seem to be a big deal by the time you picked me up so it wasn't worth talking about. I've had a really weird day and it wasn't on my mind at that point."

"These headaches *are* a big deal, Seef. What possibly could have happened that took your mind off that?"

Seefer thought about the rats, the curious new janitor and all of his extraordinary gizmos. At the expense of sounding ridiculous, or worse, dishonest, Seefer chose to stay mum.

"I guess nothing," he said.

"Well, I need to know about be these things. I shouldn't have to hear it from a note."

"But I'm okay. It's like it didn't happen."

"But it *did* happen, Seefy."

"Can you stop calling me that? I hate 'Seefy.' It's bad enough I get tormented on the bus and in school with dumb names. I should be able to talk to my mom without her calling me something stupid, too."

A look of intense guilt overcame his mother's face. "I didn't know things were going bad in school. Who's calling you names?"

"Everyone! It's either 'freak' or 'spaz' or 'weirdo' or sometimes worse. I never get invited to do anything. Everyone thinks I'm a total tool. And it especially doesn't help when you're blowing kisses at me from the car. You get on me for not cleaning enough, not sleeping enough, not wearing the right things. At what point can I get through my day without one person making me feel like poop?"

"Seef–" She was about to use the wrong term of endearment, but corrected herself. "Honey, you can always come to me when these things are bothering you. Do you realize this?"

He nodded but unconvincingly.

"I'm sorry I don't always have the time, or even make the time for you. I will try harder to do that. It's difficult sometimes with it being the two of us."

"I know," Seefer said. They sat quietly for a few moments eating their lunch. A thought arose in Seefer's head that he figured now was as good enough time to ask as any other. "But why is that?" he asked.

"Why is what?" she replied.

"Why is it only you and I? Where is my father?"

His mother's face lit up with shock. She didn't look prepared for a question like that. After thinking through her response, she answered him delicately. "Your father isn't from around here, honey."

"But he knows I exist, right?" he asked.

"Your location is no secret to anyone who really needs to find you," she said. Seefer's heart broke from the comment. She reached out to touch his hand and added. "You'd have to be crazy not to share in your life."

"I wish sometimes I could understand why he didn't

stay, or why he never visits," Seefer said.

"Don't trouble yourself with those thoughts. It's not worth it."

Seefer knew there was more to the story than his mother was telling. She was holding back. There must be good reasons for her to keep things this simple, he thought.

His mom changed the subject. "So getting back to the kids at school. Is there anything you want to talk about?"

"No, I want to forget about it. I can handle it fine enough, it gets frustrating sometimes."

"My ears are always open to you," his mom said.

"I know. If something is bugging me, I will let you know about it."

His mom had an introspective look on her face. Whatever she could have been thinking at that moment, she drew one important conclusion: "I think we both can try to communicate better."

7

Seefer's mom drove the car up to the front of the school. The first thing Seefer noticed upon his return was that Korvus' Science-Mobile had left. Panic struck his face. *Did the show finish already?*

"What's wrong?" his mother asked.

"Korvus the Magnificent," he said sadly. "His truck is gone. I missed the show."

"I'm sorry, kiddo. Maybe he's still here, but they had to move the van?"

"I doubt it." Seefer motioned toward the handle on the car door with a pout on his face.

"Wait a second." His mom reached into her purse and took out a wrapped alcohol pad. She opened it and then pulled Seefer's shirt toward her. She scrubbed the stain embedded into the fabric. She could see Seefer rolling his eyes and keeping watch in case anyone saw. "If you're going to insist on wearing dirty clothes, best not make it too apparent. Right?"

Seefer smiled. "Right."

He opened the car door and exited but popped his head back in to tell her, "Thanks, Mom. Love you."

She replied, "Love you, too. Have a great rest of your day."

Seefer walked toward the school entrance. There was an instance along the way where he felt very strange. A tingling sensation passed over his entire front side and moved to the back. He feared it might have been a precursor to another episode. Fortunately, the feeling passed quickly and he felt fine ascending the stairs to the school.

When he entered the main foyer, the silence struck him as very odd. Even when class was in session, it was never this quiet. He walked into the main office to report back. Mrs. Karcher wasn't at her desk. Principal Witik and Nurse Wendy were gone too. Usually, at least one of those three were in or near the main office at all times.

"Hello?" Seefer called out. He received no response. "Well, I'm not waiting around here again," he said to himself and left the office.

A promising thought crossed his mind. *What if they're not here, because everyone is still at the assembly?*

The door of the main office was only a short distance to the gym entrance. Seefer peered through the skinny little window of the door, he couldn't believe his eyes.

Empty.

He opened the door and looked around. There wasn't a soul in sight and not a noise to be heard except the echoes of each footstep Seefer took. Folding chairs were set up ready to seat the entire school. *Were they here already, or have they yet to come?* Some gum wrappers and other pocket trash lay on the floor between a few rows. *These seats have been sat in.*

The stage was set up for the Magnificent's show. A giant Jacob's Ladder towered above center stage, with lab tables stationed around the whole set. Chemistry beakers were ready on one table. There were balloons on another, sitting next to a large battery and some other electronic devices.

The stage mesmerized Seefer. The world of science never looked so appealing. He wondered why everything was abandoned. *There isn't one person guarding this stuff?* He neared the stage, getting good looks at the giant magnets on another table. When he looked up he wondered why none of these things are turned on.

Then Seefer realized that *nothing* was turned on in the school. The hallway had seemed a little dark when he first entered. There were certainly no lights in the office. Now standing in the middle of the gym, he could see that the only light being provided was from the windows above the bleachers. *What's going on here?*

Seefer started running through a checklist of oddities in his head. The school was silent and vacated. There should have been at least one person in the office. The power was off. If the assembly was over, why didn't anyone clean up?

"Hello!" he exclaimed. Only his echoes responded.

DINK! DINK! DINK!

He heard a noise like two pieces of metal clanging against each other. There were three distinct bangs. *Where did it come from?* The hallway! He ran toward the exit.

When he burst through the doors, he found what he should have expected – nothing.

"I'm starting to get concerned, people! Where are you all?"

He started walking down the hallway, keeping his ears keen to any sound that was made. He was not surprised when he passed the first classroom to see that it was empty. He passed a few more to see the same result.

When he arrived at his homeroom, he peaked in. "Yoo-hoo!"

He wandered around the room with mischievous intentions. He looked through some of the backpacks on the wall to be nosey. He found Hector's and took special interest while going through it. He found a note from Hector's mother that he read aloud, "Hector, there is an extra pair of undies in your pen pouch in case you have another accident. Love you, sweetie – Mom." Seefer laughed so hard it echoed throughout the empty classroom.

He took the opportunity to snoop through the teacher's desk, but took precaution before proceeding.

"Mrs. Cody? If this is a trap, you have to come out and tell me now!"

When nobody answered, he opened the top drawers. He saw nothing but standard school supplies in the center drawer. When he looked in the top right drawer, he found some items that were taken away from other students: packs of gum, an iPod, and Sally's diary. Then he stumbled upon a heavy-duty laser pointer that made his mouth drool. Seefer had a passion for cool geeky gadgetry and knew this one wasn't a run-of-the mill presentation assistant. This one looked like it had some muscle. After triple-checking that no one could see him, Seefer placed the laser in his pocket for safekeeping.

He looked in the big drawer at the bottom of the desk and found the mother load. There were two teacher-edition books for the subjects of science and math. His eyes lit up brighter than stars. He tore open the science book and found the answers to the next test. "A, C, D, B, C, D, A ..." he recited to himself.

DINK! DINK! DINK!

There was that noise again. Three measured clangs echoed in the hallway.

"Hello!" Seefer's tone grew more exasperated with each call out to the empty school.

"Whatever, I'm not going anywhere," he said to himself. He started to read the teacher manual again.

DINK! DINK! DINK!

Again, three measured clangs shout out, but this time a little louder. The increased volume compelled him put the book down and pop his head into the hallway.

Seefer didn't see anything. He could see all the way down to the main office in one direction, and the staircase that led to the other floors in the other.

He stepped out into the hallway, turned 360 degrees, and threw his hands up in the air. There was no one near.

"If someone is out there, it would help if you *said* something!"

DINK! DINK! DINK!

Standing in the hallway, Seefer had better position to locate the source of the sound. The first clang lured his eyes to the ceiling, where a series of pipes were hung. During the next two clangs, he could see one of the lines vibrate.

"The pipes."

Seefer cautiously walked toward the staircase at the end of the hall, keeping an eye to the ceiling the whole time. At the end of the hall, the pipes split in different directions. The one he followed turned upward toward the second floor. Seefer ascended the stairs to find where it led.

The second floor was a less familiar place for Seefer. All of the 8th graders had class up there. He hardly ever had a reason to pay a visit. The first three rooms on the left were science labs. The door to his right led to a computer lab. The rest were classrooms. Like the rest of the school, they all appeared empty.

Unsure what to do next, Seefer decided to do what he had been doing – yell into the emptiness.

"Hell–"

Immediately, a hand muzzled Seefer's mouth and dragged him into the science lab on the left. Whoever restrained him was strong. The person pulled Seefer against the interior wall of the classroom, trying to keep him quiet. Struggling for a breath, he wedged his fingers in between the hand covering his mouth. He created enough space to take in a huge gasp of air. His captor spun him around and sternly whispered, "Will you be quiet?!"

"Cassy?" Seefer was amazed by her strength and felt a little emasculated. "How did you…"

She instantly threw her finger against his lips and quietly shushed him. She then motioned for him to follow her.

Cassy quietly closed the door to the science lab and locked the knob. She crouched down on all fours, heading toward the windows. They crawled in and out of the chest-high lab tables, taking caution not to move any chairs.

Seefer thought he heard something in the hallway. *Were those footsteps?* He rose from his crawl position to see if he could spot anything through the glass on the door. Cassy yanked him by the shirt collar and pulled him down to the floor. She put her finger to her mouth as to say *shut up*.

A shadow of a person projected onto the glass of the lab door. Following closely behind, another shadow neared. Seefer and Cassy could hear them communicating, but had no idea what they were saying. Their *speech* sounded like garbled gibberish. It must have been the door distorting their voices.

The knob rotated slowly but was stopped by the locking mechanism. Seefer and Cassy breathed a sigh of relief. They wasted no opportunity to pull themselves behind the furthest lab table from the door.

The knob rapidly turned from side to side. Whoever was out there banged the door against the jamb at the same time. It would not open. The lock held and prevented any entry.

Cassy and Seefer heard more communication between the two in the hall. They peaked over the table to see what was happening. Only one of shadows remained.

"They must be leaving," Seefer whispered. As soon as he finished his sentence, the other figure returned, appearing to have something large in its hands. Seefer and Cassy fired frightened looks at one another then ducked below the table, trying to cram themselves into the storage space beneath it.

The blade of a fire ax smashed into the door's window, spraying glass pebbles across the room. Only the security wire and a few shards of glass remained in the cutout of the door. The ax recoiled and struck the wire, cutting through it like string.

A gloved hand reached through the broken window and turned the knob. The door crept open, sliding the broken pieces of window along with it.

The kids remained perfectly still. Seefer's face showed panic. He made no sounds, although everything about the situation urged him to scream. He had no idea why he was hiding or who he was hiding from. The only thing keeping him sane was his trust in Cassy. He looked at her. She held herself with cool and collection. Seefer thought that if she could keep it together, so could he.

The door thudded against the wall. Two figures walked into the room. They were covered from head to toe in odd looking costumes. They looked almost like astronaut spacesuits, but less cumbersome. The mirrored shields on their helmets concealed their faces. In fact, not one inch of them went uncovered.

Cassy whispered to Seefer, "Drones, shhhh."

They crept into the room with a simian stride. Their short and stout stature seemed to give them problems while walking inside their outfits. Despite the noise they just made, they returned to silence. One of them investigated the teacher's table, looking inside its large openings. The other went over to the supply cabinet and searched there.

Seefer's concern level doubled. He and Cassy

watched the scene unfold through electrical cutouts in the table. He knew it was simply a matter of time until these *drones* found them hiding under there. His heart pounded loudly against his chest. He gave Cassy a look as to say, *what do we do now?*

The drones were finished with the closet and teacher area. They started to sweep the room, walking around each lab table. There were only nine stations in the room so time was short.

Cassy reached into her pocket and pulled out a shiny object – a pocketknife! Seefer was about to exclaim, "Where the heck did you get that?" but Cassy placed her finger over his mouth. He shook his head and pointed to his temple as to say, *think.*

He then reached into his pocket and pulled out the laser pointer he *borrowed* from Mrs. Cody's desk. The device, encased in shiny aluminum and about the size of a coin roll, looked homemade but had the potential to do some damage.

Cassy's eyes lit up. "My laser!" she said quietly as she swiped it from Seefer. With a flip of its switch, she projected a violet light against the interior of the cubby. The lit area smoked instantly.

Cassy then aimed the pointer through one of the electrical cutouts. She had her sights set on the gas feed that supplied the Bunsen burners. The hose lit up with a purple glow and started to singe.

The drones were getting closer to them. Despite one of them being only a table away, Cassy's use of the laser went unnoticed.

The closer of the two stepped within inches of the kids' table. *C'mon! Work! They're going to find us!* A patch of lining surrounding the hose melted away. As the rubber shell liquefied and ran down the length of the hose, some of the fabric mesh underneath began to smoke. This caught the attention of one the drones. He yelled out some garbled command to his partner. They both stared at the smoking hose, but neither looked for the purple light's source.

Flames burst out from behind the smoke. The ruptured hose let loose a steady stream of methane, producing a two foot flame.

The distraction worked. The drones' full attention was fixed on the flame. They walked over to investigate.

Cassy whispered to Seefer, "Follow me."

Seefer figured he was better off following than staying. They slid open the door on the table and crawled toward the teacher's desk. Between the whistling gas leak and an argument between the two prowlers, there was enough noise in the room to mask the sound of their shuffling feet.

The two drones squabbled in their garbled speak. *Was the spacesuit distorting their speech, or did they really speak like that?* After assessing the situation, one of them had enough. He pulled the hose out from the table, which cut the gas supply to the flame and extinguished it. The whistling noise continued because the leak moved from the tabletop to the feed below.

This wasn't any concern to the prowlers. They resumed their search. Now slightly irritated, they tipped over tables instead of calmly investigating them. Seefer watched as they ripped the table top off the one they were hiding in. They discovered the laser pointer. They looked at it for a moment, but then tossed it to the side. Seefer breathed a sigh of relief.

After not finding what they were looking for, the drones exited the room. Seefer and Cassy waited until their steps faded before emerging from their hiding place.

"I think they're gone," Cassy said. She got up and immediately went over to the gas valve to turn it off.

Seefer opened a window. "Yuck, stinks like gas in here!" He then walked over to their original hiding spot, one that was somewhat destroyed. He saw the laser pointer on the ground. "Phew!"

"Do not turn that thing on until this room clears," Cassy warned.

Seefer froze. That was exactly the first thing he wanted to do; he never considered the gas. "Good call."

Cassy moved over to the door to make sure the hall was clear, and then returned to the window side of the room. She methodically scanned the outside and the windows themselves.

"Cassy, what's going on? Who were those guys?" Seefer asked.

Cassy was too occupied by other things. She barely acknowledged Seefer's question. Instead she tried to figure out how to disable the safety mechanism on the window.

Seefer didn't recognize this girl in his presence. While the face was the same, his goofy gal pal had disappeared. He wondered what could have been so important that she was ignoring him.

"Cass? What are you doing?"

She snapped at him. "I'm trying to find you a way out of here!"

8

"Why *me*?!" Seefer shouted.

"Keep…your…voice…down!" Cassy insisted. She continued searching the room for things to use.

"Cassy. I came back and everyone was gone. No lights. No sounds. Well, except for a banging noise that led me up here. And then I see you of all people seconds before God-knows-who turns this science lab into a disaster area."

Cassy paused to take in what Seefer said to her. "It was me, the one making that noise. I watched as you came back into the school. I was trying to lead you up here without giving myself away."

"Why? Cassy, I have NO idea what's going on! Who were those guys?"

"They came with Korvus. They are like his assistants, but he referred to them as 'drones.'"

"But why do we need to get out of here?"

"They are looking for you, Seefer!"

His jaw dropped in disbelief. "What? What are you

talking about?"

Cassy spoke with determination. "I am not pushing your leg, Seefer. They are after you and I am going to get you out of here. Once I do, I will explain more clearly."

"Pulling." Seefer cleared his throat. "It's *pulling* your leg."

Cassy rolled her eyes and continued with her escape plan. She handed Seefer a pair of pliers. "See those hex-screws above the window? Twist them out."

Seefer didn't argue. "Alright."

Cassy walked back over to the busted classroom door. She popped her head out into the hallway before walking out completely. A few moments later she returned, dragging a large fire hose behind her.

"Almost done?" she asked.

With a few more twists of the pliers, he unscrewed the last fastener. "Yeah. What are you doing with that hose?"

Cassy pulled the hose up to the window and dropped it to the floor. "We are going to get out of here."

As Cassy went about removing the window from its frame, Seefer expressed his reservations with the idea. "You know, Cass, I went through the front door pretty easily before…"

"You were lucky then. Surely, they are downstairs now. Too risky to go back."

Seefer looked at the formidable two-story drop. "You're right. We wouldn't want to be risky."

Cassy picked up the hose and hurled it out the window. The nozzle made a *THUNK* on the ground. "Perfect. Come on, Seefer, you first."

"I thought it was ladies first," Seefer said with a gulp.

"Not where I am from."

Cassy prodded Seefer onto the ledge. He carefully grabbed onto the hose and looked out the open window. Twenty feet spanned between him and the ground. He thought about how one slip of his fingers would lead to a broken leg.

"Go already!" Cassy said.

Seefer put his legs out the window and inched himself off the ledge. Taking steps along the vertical wall and moving hand-below-hand on the hose, he descended slowly toward the ground.

Seefer could feel sweat pooling in the palms of his hands. He feared it would lead to him slipping, but he couldn't wipe them off on his shirt. He crawled downward about eight feet and then used the first floor windows as his footing. The glass plates were not as stable as the brick above them.

He desperately wanted to get through this and touch the ground. With about eight more feet to go, he placed his foot onto the window in front of him. It swung open into the classroom. Seefer lost his balance and his grip on the hose. He fell the rest of the way until crashing onto the school's front lawn.

"Seefer!" Cassy yelled. "Are you okay?"

He flashed her a thumbs up. When he rolled away from the end of the hose, Cassy repelled down with the skill of a SWAT team member.

Seefer remembered Cassy trying to climb the ropes in the gymnasium during a September Phys. Ed. class. Coach Wilhelm graded all of the students on how fast or high they could climb the ropes. Like Seefer, Cassy struggled mightily to go upward. She lost her grip and fell six feet onto her rump. That display put her toward the bottom of the athletic pack, where Seefer was very used to being.

"Been practicing?" Seefer said coyly. At this point, little surprised him about Cassy's sudden metamorphosis.

She ignored the remark and pulled Seefer lower to the ground. "Stay low. Remember, they are somewhere on the first floor." Seefer looked up at the windows to make sure he wasn't being watched while Cassy crouched down into a three-point stance.

"What are you doing?" Seefer asked.

"Follow me."

Cassy burst into a full sprint heading toward the road. Seefer quickly sprang to catch her. Running as fast as he could, he still struggled to keep up. They ran across the front lawn of the school, through the parking lot and onto the road.

Cassy stopped once she reached the road. Seefer, huffing and puffing, slowed to a jog before meeting up with her.

"I think we are okay," she said. "Did you feel that? Somewhere near the lawn. Exhilarating! It was like a bolt of adrenaline! We should keep moving." She crossed the street and walked away from the school.

Seefer didn't follow.

"What are you doing? Come on!" Cassy commanded.

"No. Not until you let me know what's going on!" Seefer exclaimed.

"Alright, while we move." The two walked away from the school as Cassy told Seefer what he had missed.

"When Korvus first arrived at the school, we all got a good look at him exiting his vehicle. While everyone was marveling at the first sight of him, I grew suspect. I had seen his face before. I created a distraction to get out of class so I could feed my curiosity."

"That's why you went mental about the metric system?" Seefer asked.

"Yes, but – I spoke no falsities. The imperial system is exhausting. That is beside the point. When I was sent to the principal's office, I took the opportunity to hide out in the press box above the gym. I watched through drawn shades as Korvus set up his stage.

"To my disappointment, or perhaps my relief,

nothing out of the ordinary happened until the show began. I had already perched myself up in the cafeteria, so I was not able to rejoin the class. That was fortunate.

"The show began with dazzling lights and music thumping through the packed gymnasium. The entire school watched with full attention. A pretend spaceship landed on the stage, and a puff of smoke shot out. A hatchway door opened, and a dozen of those mirror-faced men, the drones, exited. The crowd cheered. Then the spaceship melted away to reveal Korvus. The kids went berserk."

Seefer listened with disappointment on his face. "Awww, man. Sounds awesome so far."

"He started with a segment revolved around a Jacob's ladder. He was absorbing electricity from its stack. He raised a boy's hair straight up from his head with crackling electric current. The audience was hooked. That is when he introduced his last segment."

"Last?" Seefer asked.

"Korvus addressed the crowd: 'For our next segment, I am going to need volunteers.' About every student raised his or her hand. Delighted by the response, Korvus instructed the crowd to look at the stage. A large ring descended from the ceiling. When it activated, it began distorting the air around it. That is when I had to stop watching."

"Why?" Seefer asked.

"It was not a science experiment at all. It was a very powerful and very large hypnotic device, called a *halo*.

They are usually the size of a wall clock, but this one was at least three meters in diameter, large enough to mesmerize a thousand people at once."

"Never heard of one before," Seefer said.

"They are top secret," Cassy said with a shift in her eyes. "With good reason, too. After thirty seconds of activation, the entire school was hypnotized. As a test, Korvus told everyone to look under their seats and find the envelope he placed there. He instructed to open them and remove the large sewing needle inside each one. Then he commanded everyone to insert the needle through the palm of their opposite hand."

"Ga! That's disgusting!"

"Yet no one flinched at the command. Every person in that gym obeyed. Korvus' drones walked around to ensure that they all stuck themselves. When they realized there were no dissenters amongst the crowd, they filed them out of the gym toward the athletic fields."

"Where?"

"I am not sure exactly. I could not follow without being seen myself. When two of the drones branched off from the others, I knew they would be searching for stragglers. I had to find a better hiding place."

Seefer stopped walking and tried to get his mind around the whole concept. He shook his head to see if that helped make it more swallowable.

"Okay. So those guys in the spacesuits were trying to find stragglers in the school? Why did you make such a big deal about getting *me* out there before yourself?"

"Because you are my friend?" Cassy said with an increasing tone. When Seefer nodded and accepted the answer, Cassy breathed a sigh of relief. "Besides, I can take very good care of myself."

"Yeah, that's another thing. When did you become a super-ninja warrior?"

"I guess I always had it in me," Cassy offered.

Seefer still tried to make sense of it all, but ran out of questions to ask. "Well, I still don't really know *why* all these weird things are happening, but we've got to do something to stop them, right? Isn't that like kidnapping or something?" Seefer started in the other direction, heading back toward the school.

"What do you mean? Where are you going?" Cassy asked.

Seefer said with simplicity, "The police station."

9

The Camden Police Station was situated in the heart of town, blocks away from Harrison Middle School. The modestly sized headquarters neighbored some small businesses on Camden's main street. One could easily walk by without knowing it was there.

Determined to get there quickly, Seefer hastily walked down the sidewalk. He found a sudden sense of duty that had him ignoring obstacles such as newspaper stands and pedestrians. Cassy struggled to keep up with him, as people were getting in her way to avoid colliding with Seefer.

"Can you slow down?" Cassy asked as they came upon the building. "Are we sure we even want go in there?"

Seefer stopped and turned to Cassy. "Why wouldn't we?"

"We could get in trouble," she suggested.

"How so?"

"We are playing hockey."

"Hooky. I'll take my chances." With that, Seefer walked up the stairs that led into the station.

The lobby doors swung open, and Seefer entered the welcome area. Looking straight ahead, he could see many uniformed officers working diligently in their cubicles. A wooden half-wall separated them from the lobby. Benches to the left and right provided seats for those who were waiting. A few seats were occupied by questionable characters. Seefer avoided eye contact.

A blue line on the floor led to a welcome desk. A surly old cop who looked like he treated his job as a punishment sat there with a toothpick in his mouth and a cigarette pack showing through his breast pocket. He looked like he was impatiently waiting for his next break.

The cop looked Seefer up and down, then unenthusiastically waved him over. Cassy entered right behind Seefer and followed his path. The cop suspected some tomfoolery in his midst.

"Shouldn't you two be in school?" the cop interrogated.

"See?" Cassy whispered over to Seefer.

Seefer drummed up his nerve and spoke truthfully even though his words would probably sound ridiculous. "Sir, there is nowhere that I would like to be right now more than school. Under the circumstances, we had to flee. Everyone has been kidnapped!"

The cop dropped his mouth and his toothpick. "Just a minute."

He stood up from his chair and walked over to one of the desks in the police work area. A younger officer listened to what the older cop had to say. He made the occasional glance over to the kids while hearing the story.

The younger officer came into the lobby and greeted Seefer and Cassy. They watched as the older cop walked out a side door tapping on his cigarette pack.

"Hi, I'm Officer Booth. There's a problem at school?"

"Everyone was taken! They were all hypnotized and marched away by their captor," Seefer said.

Cassy held her hand to her brow, looking slightly embarrassed by Seefer's valor.

Booth held a snicker back behind his patchy mustache. "That sounds very serious. Why don't you come over to my desk?" Booth held open the swing door on the half wall so the pair could enter.

Cassy grabbed Seefer's arm and held him back. "He does not believe you."

Seefer freed his arm. "Tell him what you know. Stop being so stubborn!"

They followed Officer Booth to his desk and took a seat. Booth grabbed a pad and pen. "Names?"

"I'm Seefer Elliot, and this is Cassy Smith."

Officer Booth recorded the information and then said, "Start from the beginning. What is going on?"

Seefer started. "I returned to school…"

"Where were you? What school?"

"I was at the doctor's. I came back to Harrison Middle. And it was completely empty. No one was there. There was supposed to be this big assembly but everyone was gone. Then I found Cassy upstairs before these men in spacesuits."

"Spacesuits?" Booth asked.

"They looked like spacesuits. I don't know. Costumes. They were part of this show that came to our school. I guess they're called 'drones.' They started tearing up the school looking for us. We escaped and came here."

"Drones? How do you know they were looking for you?"

Cassy shrugged and cooperated with a response. "I was there from the beginning. There was a man name Korvus–"

"That with a *K*"?

"Yes. He came to our school today for entertainment. He was supposed to conduct experiments that would excite the crowd. Instead he hypnotized everyone with a large device called a *halo*."

Officer Booth raised an eyebrow. "So why weren't you hypnotized?"

"I was not in the gymnasium during the performance. I was in the press booth. After I knew it was safe to look, I watched as he commanded everyone to harm themselves as a way to weed out any pretenders. Then he sent his assistants, the drones, out to hunt down any stragglers like myself."

"Why would someone do this?" Booth questioned.

"He is looking for someone. Someone very special," Cassy said.

Booth squinted his eyes in suspicion of his visitors, but something propelled him to hit the speaker button on his phone, bringing up a dial tone. He then dialed '0'. While he waited, he turned to his computer and started typing the word "Korvus" into a search engine. The screen filled up with news articles and profiles that matched the name.

Someone picked up on the other side of the phone, "Operator."

"Yes, can I get through to Harrison Middle School, please?" Booth requested.

Seefer shook his head knowing it was a waste of time. The school was empty. No one would be able to pick up, but then someone did.

"Harrison Middle School. Can I help you?"

Seefer and Cassy looked at each other with surprised eyes. *Who is that answering the phone?*

"Yes, this is Officer Booth with Camden P.D. We've had a report of some strange things happening over at the school today. Could you confirm this?"

"We have had some technical difficulties with our PA system, yes. Very frustrating. That is all."

Seefer recognized the voice. *Pavo!*

Officer Booth heard enough. "Thank you very much. Sorry to bother you." He disconnected the phone.

"No, wait!" Seefer tried to stop him.

"What's the matter?" Booth asked.

"That was the janitor. He's probably in on it."

Cassy piped up, "He is right, sir. I saw him speaking to Korvus before the incident. He is likely involved."

"Kids, I want to show you something." Officer Booth turns his computer monitor toward them. "These are all of the local search results that I turned up with 'Korvus' as a keyword. News articles raving about his performances at many area schools. No allegations of foul play. No conspiracies about kidnap or harmful manipulation. Is there any chance you misunderstood what you saw?"

Cassy responded, "Don't you see? He can hypnotize a crowd to believe anything. He could make them chop off their arms and think nothing of it."

"And when all of those armless kids go home, don't you think their parents would have something to say?" Booth offered. "Maybe write at least a few negative Internet comments?"

Seefer and Cassy had no response.

"I'll tell you what," Booth said. "I'll escort you back to school before you get into any trouble. If there's any chance your story checks out, I'll be right there to take care of the problem."

Seefer and Cassy looked at each other then nodded to Booth.

"Okay. Follow me." Booth led them out of the work area and back through the lobby. When they passed the welcome desk, the old surly cop was sitting there again. "I'm taking these kids back to school."

The old cop responded as the trio left the station, "I'll be sure to wait up for you."

The kids packed into Booth's police cruiser. Seefer had always wanted to ride in one before, and under any other circumstance would be excited by this chance. Other thoughts raced through his mind at that moment – thoughts about what to expect in the next few minutes. While they didn't want to be proven wrong once they arrived at the school, they surely didn't want to reencounter the drones.

The ride to the school was short. When they pulled into the front parking lot, nothing had changed. The power was still out and the fire hose they used earlier remained hanging from the second story window.

Booth turned to Seefer and Cassy. They had dreadful looks on their faces since they moment they arrived. "Okay, we're here." He exited his door and let them out of the back seat.

"Officer, do you see that hose?" Seefer pointed out the one hanging out the window. "That is what we used to escape."

The hose piqued Booth's interest. Seeing it gave credibility to the story he heard at the police station. "Why don't you walk behind me?" Booth suggested. He unclipped the strap on his holster, but left his gun in place. He slowly walked up the path toward the school. Seefer and Cassy followed close behind. They walked four steps when…

B-ZAP!

…a giant burst of energy shot out from nowhere and smacked Officer Booth ten feet backwards. He landed horizontally and knocked his head on the sidewalk.

Seefer froze. *Is he dead?* As he looked at Booth's motionless body, he repeatedly muttered, "This is not happening." He didn't know what to do. He'd never seen a person rendered unconscious before by such a violent action. He back pedaled away from Booth's body, both out of fear and caution, but did not realize that he crossed the same spot that produced the energy burst.

Cassy rushed over and examined Booth. She touched him on the neck looking for a pulse. She found one and smiled. "Hey Seefer, he is alive!" When she looked up, she found him backed up half way to the school.

"Seefer, what are you doing? Come back!" She yelled.

He didn't hear her. Still dazed by what occurred, he

paid no attention to Cassy's words. The timing could not be worse. One of Korvus' drones charged out of the school entrance and headed right for him. Seefer didn't see him coming. The drone grabbed Seefer in a headlock and dragged him backwards.

"Seefer!" Cassy shouted. She ran after him without any hesitation.

When she was close enough, Cassy leapt into the air and delivered a kick to the drone's head, cracking his mirrored faceplate. This action freed Seefer for the moment, but he didn't use the opportunity to escape. Cassy regained her stance on the steps of the school, between the entrance and the drone.

The drone gathered himself and adjusted his fractured helmet. He ignored Seefer for the moment and focused on Cassy, who cracked her knuckles and egged him to come hither. Before the two could wage battle, another drone grabbed Cassy from behind and pulled her inside. Her apologetic eyes fixed on Seefer as the henchman dragged her into the shadows of the school.

Caught off guard by her capture, Seefer failed to dodge the remaining drone's grab at him. The brutish henchman threw Seefer over his shoulder and walked in close behind the other.

When they entered, a surprise awaited. Cassy's captor was out cold on the ground while she fixed herself up. She looked up at the drone holding Seefer and gave him a girlish wave.

The henchman tossed Seefer to the side and

approached Cassy with the stride of a wolf. Only an instance later, his face met the force of a large blunt object, sending him to the floor.

The drone tried to get up, but a foot stomped on his chest. Pavo held a mop high in the air and drove its handle into the mirrored faceplate of the drone.

Pavo took out a rag from his pocket and wiped his brow. His predator-on-the-attack demeanor quickly changed to a calmer, more collective one as he surveyed the scene. Seefer and Cassy watched in bewilderment. *What's he going to do to us now?*

Pavo motioned to both of them to come closer. They treaded carefully, but honored the request. Pavo hunched over, and in a very disappointed tone, said, "You two should not have returned."

10

Seefer and Cassy stared into Pavo's scolding eyes. Being so close, Seefer couldn't help but look over the scars and pockmarks covering Pavo's face. His skin spoke volumes about a history of battle and hand-to-hand combat.

"What are you going to do with us?" Cassy asked demandingly.

Pavo laughed. "What am *I* going to do with you?"

Cassy challenged him. "You and Korvus were colluding earlier. I saw you speak with him before the assembly."

"Yes, you are correct. I spoke with him earlier in the gymnasium. He only needed the help of a lowly janitor. I cooperated only to keep Korvus from seeing him." Pavo held his hand out toward Seefer.

Cassy turned to Seefer looking for confirmation. Seefer nodded and said, "He did push me out of the way so Korvus couldn't see me."

"Pushed you?!" Pavo said, taking offense. "I am on

your side."

"Prove it!" Cassy demanded.

Pavo pointed to the unconscious henchmen on the floor. "Did you not see what I did here? How many more would convince you?"

"But every weird thing that's happened to me or this school today somehow involved you," Seefer said. "Don't you think it's a little hard to believe that you're on our side?"

"Like what?" asked Pavo.

Seefer rattled off his list, "The weird PA noises, your high tech gizmos, the crazy rats, you pricking me in your dungeon lair!"

"Those were all tests meant to find you, young one. My equipment seemed to be incompatible with some of the building's wiring, hence the interference noise." Pavo said to Seefer.

Cassy leered at Pavo with disbelief. "Why would *you* be looking for him?"

"Because," Pavo explained, "if Korvus found him first, it would mean the end of us all."

A long pause occurred after Pavo's admission. Finally, Seefer broke the silence with his most honest reaction. "Whaaaaat?"

Pavo kept his response simple. "If you can trust me enough for me to lead you away from this school, I will explain everything."

Seefer and Cassy agreed to trust him, but there was

something they had to deal with first. "What about Officer Booth? We can't leave him out there like that," said Seefer.

Pavo considered the statement and agreed.

The three went outside and examined the unconscious policeman. "How did this happen?" Seefer asked.

"There is a perimeter shield around the entire school," Pavo explained. "This policeman walked right into it."

"Shouldn't we have been knocked unconscious, too? This is the third time we crossed this lawn."

"Most likely it has been set with *certain* restrictions. The two of you must have met the acceptance criteria."

"What criteria?"

Pavo deflected the question. "Come. We need to return this man to his vehicle." Pavo grabbed Booth from under his arms, and the kids each took a leg. They carried him over to the police cruiser parked in front of the school.

Pavo situated Booth's body in the driver seat and reclined the chair slightly. Cassy helped pull him through from the other side. Pavo saw a newspaper on the passenger seat. "Hand me that," he said to Cassy. He sprawled the paper open on Booth's chest.

When they were through, they created the illusion of Booth falling asleep while reading in his car.

"Now we must get you out of here," Pavo said.

"We can go to my house," Seefer offered.

"No, we can go to mine," Cassy said. "It is closer and I can guarantee no one will be there."

"Who would possibly be at my house?" Seefer asked.

"You do have a mother, do you not?" Cassy asked sarcastically.

"Uh, yeah. Don't you?"

Cassy did not respond.

"Right?" Seefer checked.

"We go to the girl's house." Pavo said assertively. "There is much to discuss."

11

Stuffed inside the school's groundskeeper cart, the band of unlikely allies arrived at Cassy's house. The cape-styled home did not invite any guests to come knocking. The shades on every window were drawn shut. The landscaping was overgrown and unattended. From the perspective of a passerby, the place looked deserted.

"This is it," Cassy announced.

Seefer feigned enthusiasm. "Oh, nice place, Cass."

"You are certain no one is inside?" Pavo asked.

"No one that I am expecting," Cassy assured.

"Then best we get on with it," Pavo said.

The three entered the house. Upon entering, Pavo and Seefer found the interior most unusual, but to Cassy it was her safe haven.

"Home sweet home," Cassy said.

"Much roomier than I expected," Seefer said. He stared straight upward and fixed his eyes on the roof rafters twenty feet above him. There was no second floor and no walls besides the exterior ones that were undecorated and coated in a bland off-white paint. The inside resembled a giant barn rather than a home.

A functional but inhospitable kitchen awaited the group in front of the entrance. Training equipment such as gymnastic rings, weights and dummy weapons aligned the walls like a dojo. Ropes, not unlike the ones at school, suspended from the roof.

"So this is your secret," Seefer said as he twirled one of the ropes.

Pavo wasted no time. He addressed Cassy, "Girl, is there a place we can sit?"

Cassy scowled at the address. "I have a name, so you know…"

"It would be best to refrain from familiarity," said Pavo.

"If that is what you want…janitor." Cassy led Seefer and Pavo over to a worn couch near the kitchen. Pavo gestured to have a seat.

"I owe you answers," Pavo started. He grabbed a marker from his shirt pocket and walked over to the wall. He drew two horizontal squiggles on the wall.

"Excuse me! My walls?" Cassy exclaimed.

Seefer nudged Cassy and prompted her to look around at the mess she lived in. "Really?"

"This is time. Imagine it flowing left to right like a river." Pavo then wrote with his marker, *30 Okt, 1961.* "Do you know what happened on this date?" He drew a pronounced dot on the right end of the two wavy lines.

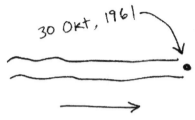

Seefer already lost interest. He felt like he was in history class. Cassy knew the answer but had the enthusiasm of someone who had answered the question a thousand times.

"Tsar Bomba," she said flatly.

Pavo responded, "Correct. The Soviet Union detonated a nuclear device on an island in the Arctic Ocean. Your history books will mark its significance by stating that it was the largest detonation in the history of this planet and how it fit into the grand scheme of the Cold War."

Seefer grew slightly more interested, but he couldn't help being slightly uncooperative. "So that's how the entire school went missing? Got it!"

Pavo ignored the sarcasm and continued. "Your books will not contain the astrophysical effects that happened on that day." From the date point he drew two sets of squiggles that branched out in new directions. "That blast yielded more energy than anyone here realized. So much that it ruptured the time continuum."

"Huh?" Seefer said.

"Simply put, since 1961, there have been two planet Earths. We identify them as being Alpha, the domain which you are familiar with, and Omega. They are actually the same Earth. They have the same histories, but vastly different futures from this point on." Pavo explained while emphasizing the date point on his diagram.

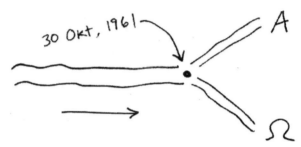

"Uh..." Seefer wasn't following.

"Tsar Bomba's yield was meant to be ten times larger than what was recorded. It was an arrogant experiment of human desire to be bigger and stronger than anyone else. When the detonation occurred, analysts here, in Alpha, measured its yield to be *only* 57 megatons. Where do you think the rest of that energy went?"

I don't know. "Space?"

Pavo circled the area of his diagram around the dot. "In some ways, but the energy actually shredded space – and time – so much that our continuum split in two. The Omega domain received the remainder of the yield, which was recorded to be over 200 megatons. That was enough to destroy the entire western shore of the detonation site."

Seefer stared at the diagram with confusion. "I've never heard about any of this before."

"No surprise," said Pavo. "No one here realized it occurred. Your historical records report that researchers redesigned the bomb in order to reduce the yield. That is false. The design was never changed. I am sure scientists close to the test had their theories on why their bomb yielded a fraction of the intended energy production, but those theories have never been heard outside of that research facility. For everyone else, the bomb, although the biggest ever made, was just another bomb being tested in a world mad with destroying itself.

"In Omega, the world took notice of the Tsar Bomba detonation because of its magnitude. An island was nearly wiped off the face of the planet. The disaster forced humans globally to rethink the future of the Cold War and the use of nuclear weapons. The world's superpowers reached agreements to disarm all of their nuclear weapons."

Cassy nodded along with the story. Seefer scratched his head. "So can I get this straight? You're telling me that there's a completely different planet Earth out there, and it's different because the big bomb had an even bigger blast on one side than the other?"

"Precisely! That was the start of it. Then came the Visitation."

Seefer looked inquisitively. "The what?"

"Do you know what radiation does in space?" Pavo asked.

"No."

"It keeps traveling until something stops it – no different than light. In 1961, the Alpha bomb created a cloud that reached the lower mesosphere. In Omega, the cloud rose into the thermosphere, almost double the height. These clouds are simply water vapor and debris. They eventually settle back to Earth. Light and radiation do not. They keep going. You can imagine how much greater the radiation created by the Omega bomb was. The greater the yield, the further it can travel in space. And the further it travels, the more likely someone will see it."

"Like who?" Seefer asked with extreme interest.

"Though it took years, someone eventually saw the radiation produced by the Omega bomb – a race of beings we on Earth called the Gliesians," Pavo answered.

Seefer started laughing. "Aliens?! Let me guess, they're little grey men with big black eyes!"

Despite the mockery, Pavo began to answer, "As a matter of fact…"

Cassy interrupted in a calm voice, "Seefer, listen to him." He suddenly felt guilty for ridiculing the thought and agreed to listen.

Pavo continued, "Even though the explosion may seem immense, it could never be detected from the Gliesian home planet. However, a Gliesian starship scouting the outer reaches of our solar system detected the radiation and charted a course toward Earth to investigate."

"In 1968, they landed near Moscow. Government leaders and brilliant scientists from all over met with the visitors. A great exchange of information occurred."

"The following decades produced the greatest Renaissance in human history, giving birth to an age of science and reason. Humans put the world's divisive issues like money, government and religion to the side in order to work *together*. Our economies were based on necessity instead of luxury. Medicine cured horrible diseases while lifestyle improvements stabilized the population. No human went hungry, homeless or without education."

Seefer is stuck on one detail. "Okay, so, if that's all true, why didn't they visit this Earth?"

Pavo answered, "The yield of the Alpha bomb was not large enough. Its energy did not signal the Gliesians like it did in Omega."

Seefer looked at Cassy. "You're okay with all of this? You haven't said much."

"It is nothing I have not heard already, Seef." Cassy said.

Seefer looked at her strangely. *What's that supposed to mean?* There was so much going on in his head he didn't know where to aim his thoughts. He listened to what should have been a highly unbelievable fantasy story about aliens visiting the Earth, but it was delivered with such matter-of-factness, he started to believe.

"So. How do *you* know all of this? I'm sorry, but aren't you just a janitor?" Seefer asked hesitantly.

Pavo smiled. "I am a janitor, but I was a soldier. And I fought the Gliesians when they turned on us."

Seefer clenched his head. "I should have known there was more."

"At the turn of the century, humans and Gliesians initiated their joint effort in building a space portal. The Gliesians who were here wanted to bridge their old home with their new. The distance of twenty light years was much too far for any conventional travel. Even the scout vessel that landed in 1968 had been traveling for centuries before coming anywhere near Earth.

"A brilliant woman named Vela led a team of scientists on the project. Her contributions catapulted the Gliesian technology to new heights. Without her, the portal would never have been feasible. Unfortunately, it had its setbacks.

"The channel required two endpoints, one on Earth and one on the alien world. The connection of these gates would allow anyone or anything to travel between them. This was the concept at least. The execution did not prove to be as successful.

"The first test was a disaster. An envoy entered the gate from our planet, but never made it through. Our constantly expanding universe shredded the channel and those inside it. Twenty light years was too far a gap to bridge.

"Vela worked diligently to find a solution. Even with the help of the most brilliant physicists, chemists, and engineers, no one could find a way. Not until a neurologist, Neils, suggested a different approach. Studying principles long regarded as fringe theories, the scientists tapped into the potential of the human mind. Eventually, they found a way for a human to uphold the channel – an overly developed mind that could balance out the gravitational forces trying to pull the universe apart."

Seefer interrupted, "You're losing me again."

Pavo seemed frustrated by his lack of understanding. "Public schools," he sighed. "They needed someone who could keep the tunnel open so people could travel between Earth and the Gliesian home world."

"Oh, why didn't you just say that?" Seefer said wryly.

"They could not bestow anyone with this ability. The person that received it would have to grow with it – all the way from a single strand of DNA. Vela trusted the only person she could with the child that would become the key to Gliese – herself.

"This approach drew the ire of Gliesians. They wanted results immediately. Gliesians were accustomed to technological advancements happening swiftly when needed. Their desperation roused the suspicion of many humans close to the effort. Why did they care so much about getting home?"

"I dunno," Seefer answered.

"That was rhetorical. Spies uncovered communications sent to the Gliese star system twenty-two years prior – enough time for their home world to receive the message and prepare for an Exodus. The portal was in their plans all along.

"Their star was dying and volatile. Little time was left for their world. The vessel that happened to discover Earth was searching for a new world to inhabit. They used humans to modernize our world to Gliesian standards and prepare it for their kind to take over. They would not be able to do that without the channel.

"In her research of wormholes and star gates, Vela discovered our parallel timelines, domains, as I described. She developed a way for her to travel between them. Worming through time proved to be less difficult, considering the relative position in space.

"To save humanity and her unborn child, she traveled to this domain to deliver him. Her son, Cepheus, was born here. She loved him dearly, but knew if she stayed here too, he would surely be found. She gave him up to someone who would care for him as her own. "

Seefer looked at Pavo blankly. Cassy whispered over to him, "He is talking about you."

"Huh? No way!" Seefer processed more of the facts. "Wait, so are you saying I'm adopted?"

"It is indeed a very tall tale to swallow all at once," Pavo said. "But think about this. Do strange unexplained things ever happen to you? Perhaps triggered by certain emotions?"

Seefer squinted his eyes, "Maybe."

"Have you recently experienced any changes within? Panic attacks? Migraines?"

"All the time," Seefer answered.

"It is your body adjusting to the abilities that have been embedded inside of you. They were designed to flower during your pubescent years."

"Okay, so even if I did believe all of this wackiness about aliens and space tunnels and me having crazy powers, which is all so ridiculous, why are those guys attacking the school and chasing after us?"

Pavo responded simply, "They are hunting for Cepheus, the key to Gliese."

12

Seefer sat by himself deep in thought. Five hours ago he woke up in his comfortable bed, rushing through his typical morning routine. The only thing he had to worry about was getting to the bus on time.

With knowledge comes responsibility and Seefer received a ton of each. He learned of other events and existences that were unbeknownst to him at bedtime yesterday. The world around him seemed so different so suddenly. He had many questions racing through his head, but didn't know where to begin asking.

Skepticism filled him. *How could all of this be true?* Seefer was reluctant to believe, because that would mean things would change for him. He considered running out the front door and leaving this all behind. If he didn't have to face the truth, then maybe he could live blissfully in ignorance. That option appealed to him.

Where would I go? If he trusted this stranger's word, it would mean his mom was not his mother. *Has she been deceiving me this whole time or does she not know either?* Seefer wished for his mother's presence so he could ask her, but also longed for her familiarity.

Even with Cassy present, he still felt like he was in the company of strangers. Cassy was not acting her usual self and Pavo was a total mystery. Seefer began feeling very alone.

He supposed that he always had a loner mentality. He certainly felt different around other kids, but never in a good way. Seefer never categorized that feeling as *special* like Pavo would have him believe. He often attributed the oddities that followed him as unfortunate luck or bad karma. According to Pavo, those weird happenings resulted from some suppressed power that lied dormant inside of him.

He looked over and saw Pavo and Cassy discussing things like they were old friends. *What on earth could they be talking about?*

Seefer overheard Pavo say the words, "Does he trust you?" They must have noticed he was listening because they quickly quieted their voices.

He grew frustrated that they left him alone with his thoughts and didn't seem to care enough to talk him through his worries. Seefer suspected they had ulterior motives and he wasn't going to let them conspire any longer.

He stood up from the couch and approached them. Pavo and Cassy looked surprised to see how together he was.

"I'm ready," Seefer said.

"For what?" Cassy asked.

Then Seefer thought of something. "Pavo, you said I have some abilities, right?" Pavo nodded. "What can I do?"

Pavo smiled. "So you *are* ready to believe?"

"I'd love to," Seefer replied, "but I'm gonna need some proof."

After raiding some of the household products in Cassy's half-kitchen, the trio set up an experiment on a table. Pavo poured water and dish soap into a rusty paint-roller pan. Cassy placed a wire hanger she had bent into a ring into the soapy solution. Drawing the hanger from the pan, Seefer saw what they created.

"Bubbles?"

Cassy slowly waved the ring and a large bubble developed.

Pavo instructed, "Yes, bubbles. They are such simple yet amazing constructs."

"So what am I supposed to do?" Seefer asked.

"Before you, there is a fragile layer of soapy water encasing a pocket of air. It only needs a tiny rupture to burst the entire sphere. According to my mission notes, your mind should be developed enough by now to cause that tear. Concentrate, and see if you can do it."

With a great strain upon his face, Seefer stared at the large bubble floating before him. Then *POP!* With his finger, he poked through the outer shell. "Oh look at me. I'm a god!" Seefer joked.

Cassy rolled her eyes, "Very funny."

"Thankees," he replied in a silly voice.

Cassy smirked. That was the first time she had all day.

Pavo urged him to try again. Cassy created another large bubble.

"Focus on the orb," Pavo said. "Sense its structure. Look for the frailties in its skin. It is nothing more than molecules of soap and water bonded together in a simple solution. Can you see them?"

Cassy created some more. There were bubbles all around.

Pavo continued, "Do not get caught on the outward beauty of the whole. Ignore the colors swimming along the surface. They are but mere distractions. Look deeper. Think smaller. Your mind will guide you. Your eyes can only see so far."

Seefer closed his eyes and *felt* the bubble as Pavo encouraged.

"Do you sense any movement? Not just the bubble descending in air, but within itself."

Seefer did. He could sense *something* coming from the bubbles, though the feeling was vague. "I…I think so."

"All matter is made up of tiny particles called *atoms*. You have the unique ability to observe the vibrations that are emitted from them. All matter is in a constant state of motion, though we cannot see that motion. We only see solid or liquid. What you are sensing now is matter in its real, not perceived, state."

As Seefer beheld the vibrations emanating from the bubbles' structure, Pavo added one more instruction. "Now try with all of your concentration to destroy them."

"What? Why?"

"Because that is what you are designed to do," Pavo said.

He aimed his thoughts at one of the bubbles. The vibration of its particles dazzled Seefer. *How could I shred apart a bubble? These things won't stop vibrating. What if they did? What if they vibrated faster?*

Seefer imagined the particles inside the bubble solution speeding up and slowing down. He envisioned the atoms moving apart from one another. Unfortunately, none of these thoughts produced results. Until…

THUMP!

Cassy whacked a book against the table, startling Seefer. "What did you do that for? I was so close!"

Cassy laughed, "Not as close as you are now!"

Seefer hadn't noticed but every bubble had burst simultaneously with the book slam.

"The book popped them all?" he asked.

"No. You did it, young one," Pavo informed him.

"Sometimes concentrating too much can lead you astray. Let us take a different approach. Can you tell me about all of the strange, unexplained things you have experienced in recent months?"

Seefer rattled off a list. He spoke of everything from the urinal flushers in September to the alarm clock and bus breakdown that very morning.

"Do you see a pattern?" Pavo asked. "Those events stemmed from your sub conscience. You need to find the right trigger, the right motivation. Whether it is sadness, anger, or fear, your body has found a means to release the negative energy and manifest it into something else. When trying to repeat the effect, you must replicate the cause."

"Hmm. So what if I'm not feeling any of those things right now?" Seefer asked.

"Then get mad!" exclaimed Pavo. "Cassy, more bubbles!"

Cassy created a sea of bubbles with her wire. Seefer resumed his exercise. He watched Cassy's wired wand glide across her body as air passed into the inflating bubble, the solution stretching thinner until it released from the wire and formed the bubble. There was movement everywhere.

Seefer focused on the most recently formed bubble and executed the mental exercise given to him. Pavo wanted him to get mad, but that wasn't exactly easy. He wasn't mad at anyone or anything at the moment.

He started thinking about the events of the day:

almost being kidnapped, having an explosive headache in front of his classmates, and being ridiculed as *rat boy*. None of those seemed to get his blood boiling. He thought of Hector's relentless attempts to belittle him, like this morning after Seefer had missed the bus or in the locker room. Hector's insults had become so commonplace; Seefer was more surprised on days when Hector had *nothing* to say.

He thought about his mother getting on his case in the morning. Thinking about her constantly nagging about his clothes and preparedness set him off a twinge. She had already apologized for being harsh on him, so he found it hard to hold the grudge.

Thinking about his mother got his mind going about the story Pavo told him earlier. *Who was my mom really? Could I even call her* mom? Seefer thought about all of the times that she had gotten down on him for not being honest and truthful and trustworthy to others. He thought about how hypocritical she was to tell *him* to speak the truth. How dare she! Until today he lived under the impression that he was her son, flesh and blood. No wonder why they didn't get along that well. *She was just a glorified nanny!*

His birth mother might have had good intentions leaving him in this world, but it sounded like she did a careless thing in creating Seefer in the first place. She didn't want a son; she wanted an instrument – something to make her precious invention work.

So on a day when another child might feel doubly

wanted, Seefer suddenly felt twice abandoned. His birth mother dropped him off and disappeared into another universe. How much further away could you want to get from your son? And even though his current mom never abandoned him, she always seemed *burdened* by Seefer. Like puzzle pieces falling into place, Seefer realized that his mom perhaps took care of him more out of duty than love. *Did anyone LOVE me?*

Heavy emotions circled inside of Seefer's head – grief, feelings of betrayal, abandonment, loneliness and then anger. He was mad at his mother. *His mothers.* Mad at the world that created him. Mad at the circumstances that brought him here and made him such a disaster in his social life. Mad that, right now, he was in this stupid empty house of Cassy's concentrating on bubbles and trying to make them –

POP!

All of them, each bubble, burst simultaneously. Their soapy water remains splashed to the ground. Pavo looked on proudly. Cassy showed a revived enthusiasm.

"You did it!" Cassy exclaimed.

"Go me!" Seefer sighed with thick sarcasm.

"You tapped into your primal emotions and projected the energy outward," Pavo said. "But where was your focus?"

Seefer scoffed at the question. *Did you not see what I just did?*

Pavo continued, "Do you see the extent of your chaos? Bubbles all around the room burst, even ones you were not focusing on. That is something we will need to work on."

Can't wait. Seefer wasn't happy, feeling depressed from the negative thoughts in his head. *It's my fault I feel this way. I am the one who asked Pavo to teach me.* Even though he had to dredge up some unpleasant thoughts, the result was pretty cool.

Recognizing the scowl on Seefer's face, Cassy suggested, "Maybe we should take a break?"

"No," Seefer said. "I need to learn this."

"I like that spirit!" Pavo cheered. He dashed off to another part of the house looking for his next prop.

In Pavo's absence, Cassy asked Seefer, "Are you okay? You look distraught."

Seefer brushed off the bad vibes. "No, I'm okay. Just trying to understand things."

"It is a lot to take in, is it not?" she asked.

"Uh, yeah. You think? When are you going to start explaining some things? What were you and Pavo talking about before?"

Cassy saw Pavo returning, "The next time we are alone."

"Okay!" Pavo said returning with a pile of clutter in his arms. "Let us continue." He plopped the objects down on the table in front of the sofa.

Seefer inspected the items. "What's with this stuff?" Seefer asked.

"A collection of materials varying in weight and

size. I do not know the extent you can perform your ability. Altering the matter inside a light-weight bubble is very basic." Pavo held up a snow globe. "But could you handle something with a little more mass?"

Seefer looked over the objects: a crumpled napkin, a section of the newspaper, a can of creamed corn, a 5 lb. weight, a hammer, and snow globe. "I'll try my best."

"Start with the lightest and work your way up," said Pavo. "Gravity is relative to mass. You will need to tune your ability before moving onto bigger objects."

"Like space tunnels?" Seefer asked slyly.

"Correct."

Seefer stared at the napkin and went through the same thought process that resulted in burst bubbles. He cleared his mind until the only thing that he could sense were the objects before him. He wasn't exactly sure how his mind distinguished them, but he could sense the objects' weight and mass without touching or feeling any of them. The napkin did not *move* like the others. Its particles were not as densely packed. There was less vibration – less movement. He focused deeper on this grouping. He envisioned the atoms drawing nearer to one another.

Cassy and Pavo watched the napkin. It crumpled tighter with no apparent outside force. The outer layers of the napkin drew into the center, making it a smaller, denser ball.

"Look at that!" Cassy said with hushed amazement.

"Remarkable." Pavo agreed.

Seefer opened his eyes and beheld what he had done. While a part of him passed off the squishing of a napkin as silly, the other couldn't help but feel proud and excited by the feat. His face showed the enthusiasm.

"Baby steps, young one. You have a long way to go. Try something else." Pavo then looked at his watch. "Hmmm. We have some preparation before we can move on. You keep working on what you have learned."

Seefer turned back to his table of test subjects and eagerly began working on his next task. He set his sights on the newspaper, hoping to turn its pages.

While Seefer stayed occupied with practice, Pavo invited Cassy to sit at the table, away from the sofa. Pavo unfolded a map before her and laid out a plan. Seefer didn't pay much attention to their discussion, but he could see Pavo tracing different paths along the paper, as if plotting a route.

Seefer worked on the newspaper. He tried to build a force strong enough to lift a sheet from the rest of the stack. Unlike the exercise with the napkin, his thoughts would need to be directed at a single page, and not the entire section. No sign of progress had occurred until he overheard the phrase "We must never allow him to return to Camden" come from Pavo's mouth. Suddenly the pages in the newspaper fluttered by like they were being blown by a gust of wind.

"What was that you said?" Seefer asked about Pavo's plan.

Pavo responded with a matter-of-fact tone, "Surely you did not expect to stay here where it is unsafe. Korvus' team will find traces of your presence and you will be in absolute danger."

"But I thought you were here to protect me," Seefer pointed out.

"I am but one man. We are but three. Korvus has dozens at his disposal."

"But this is my home. I grew up here. My friends – well, my classmates are here. Does my mom know about this?"

"Of course," Pavo said.

"He means the one he knows," Cassy corrected.

"Oh," Pavo said. "Then, no. She cannot come."

Exasperated, Seefer yelled, "Well, don't I get a say in all of this?! I don't even know you! How do I know you're not a crazy kidnapper with a good story?"

"Would I not have run off with you already? You are in danger, Seefer Elliot. This world of yours is not as safe as it appears. I will protect you and guide you through it. Your future begins by us leaving here and soon."

The change of plans took Seefer by surprise. He may have followed Pavo up to this point, but leaving unannounced in the midst of the day was too ridiculous and unsettling.

"I need a minute," Seefer said.

Pavo leaned over and put his hand on Seefer's shoulder. "You have absorbed a good deal of information in this hour. Your entire life will change from this point forward. If a minute is all you need to grapple with this course of action, you go take it."

Seefer walked out of the house with a ghostly look on his face. He never once looked back at the two he left behind.

"Are you sure we must abandon his mom?" Cassy asked. "He is quite attached."

"She is traceable. If any connection between the boy and his mother is made, her entire network of associates would become a bulls-eye pointing right at us."

Cassy countered. "Bringing her along could be advantageous. A missing child report would not help the escape."

Pavo insisted, "This is not debatable. You either help execute my plan or do not participate."

Cassy sneered at him. "Who do you think you are? Your rules will have to be bent at some point. He is not like us." She stormed outside to check on Seefer, but quickly returned. She had a look of dread on her face.

Pavo exclaimed, "What is it?"

Cassy shouted, "He is gone!"

13

Seefer stood before Harrison Middle School uncommitted to his plan. He wasn't sure why he suddenly ran from Pavo and Cassy, but he knew that he couldn't stay with them. The thought of never returning to Camden, or seeing his mom again, haunted him. He could no longer trust anyone that would impose that course of action upon him.

So Seefer ran to a most illogical place – Harrison. Behind its walls waited dangerous men out to get him. Seefer didn't understand what they were capable of doing. In some ways, he didn't want to know.

He inspected the police car they left behind and saw Officer Booth still passed out in the driver seat. No one appeared to have bothered him in the meantime. Looking around, Seefer saw nothing peculiar, although at this point, he realized anything could happen.

He walked across the front lawn of the school and crossed the perimeter shield, tickling his skin. He thought that whoever set up this shield wanted him to return.

Atop the steps of the school, he pulled open the front door and slowly entered. The men they fought earlier were no longer lying on the foyer floor. *That's not a good sign.* Korvus must now know there were hostiles on the loose, and he would be looking for them.

Seefer knew better than to shout "hello" like he did the last time he entered the empty school. Instead he moved silently down the hallway without a destination in mind. Walking through the corridor and past the classrooms, reminded him of his encounter with Pavo that morning. He picked up his pace because he figured out where he would go next – the custodial room.

The basement was even darker and more uninviting than before. With the school's power still out, there was hardly enough light for Seefer to see his hands before his face.

The only trace of light came from the glow of the custodian's room. With every footstep closer to the room, Seefer's eyes adjusted to the increasing brightness.

Upon entering the room, Seefer's footsteps stirred the caged rats into a tizzy, at least those that were still alive. Seefer ignored their stirring in order to concentrate.

Daylight poured down the back staircase, providing Seefer with enough light to find the shiny metal case Pavo used earlier. Pavo had slipped it behind a raggedy curtain near the old weathered table. Seefer tried to pick it up, but was shocked how hard it was to lift.

"Got to hit the gym, Seef," he said to himself.

With another lunge he heaved it up and successfully landed it on the rickety table. Once again, it didn't look like the table legs would be able to handle the weight. Seefer ignored the creaking and shaking and worried about the case.

He didn't notice this before, but the case included a pair of locks. Four numbers on each were set to zero. Finding the correct combination would take forever.

He tried 1-2-3-4, 1-1-1-1, 2-2-2-2, and so on, but no simplistic code worked.

Dejected that his plan had completely fallen apart, Seefer shoved the case across the table. The sudden shift in weight on the surface caused the wobbly legs to fall out from beneath the tabletop. The heavy case crashed to the floor and sat atop a pile of cheap wood.

"Figures." Seefer sighed. His really bad morning had turned into an awful afternoon. There was, however, one bright spot to his crazy Monday. Seefer finally understood why he always felt so different, in the good ways and the bad. He finally found a way to deal with the imbalance he felt in his brain and use it to his advantage, even if he wasn't reshaping space and time at the moment.

Determined not to let a small thing like a combination lock get in his way, Seefer approached the case with renewed enthusiasm. As he lowered his face to the ground, he was delighted to see that the case had sprung open from the impact of his toss.

He cautiously opened the case fully and stared at the gallery of other-worldly tools before him. His eyes passed over the *stud-finder* that he became well acquainted with earlier. He steered clear of the pen and whirly thing that Pavo used earlier to sample his blood. Instead, he explored the rest of the kit.

Seefer first took out a bracelet. It was studded with platinum stones connected by a thick metal cable. On closer inspection, Seefer saw tiny blue lights embedded inside each one. He tried the bracelet on. The lights immediately gleamed.

Seefer admired the bracelet, even if it meant sacrificing his masculinity. It was cool, even stylish. When he turned his wrist over, he mistakenly clenched his fist. Suddenly, his entire body flung, wrist first, onto the ground. The bracelet whirred as it kept Seefer glued to the floor. When he relaxed his hand and opened his fist, the whirring noise stopped. He was free to lift his arm.

"I'll be keeping you," Seefer said gleefully to the bracelet.

He then pulled out a device that resembled an egg timer. Like all the other devices, it was plated in shiny silver. As Seefer held it in his hands, it felt heavier than any egg timer he'd held before, and it wasn't just because of the metal exterior.

Curious, he set the timer on the work bench across

the room. He twisted the dial and left it at the half-minute mark. Instantly, the top of the timer opened up and shone a blue light straight up to the ceiling. The room illuminated.

The beam of light started spreading and took the shape of a large funnel. The room grew brighter. Seefer eagerly anticipated what would happen next.

Ten seconds remained. The light grew brighter.

Seefer caught a shadow in the corner of his eye. Somebody walked by the staircase leading outside. When Seefer turned, the shadow was gone, but he saw the metal Bilco doors quickly slam shut. The only light was now coming from the egg timer.

Seefer brushed off the commotion on the stairs. He wanted to see this device do something awesome. Five seconds remained.

A hand grabbed Seefer's shoulder and pulled him to the ground. Seefer yelped. He fought to stand back up, but his restrainer yelled, "Stay down!"

He saw the egg timer's blue glow change to red and intensify. With a sudden surge of noise and light, it produced a blinding flash. Then as quickly as the light came on, the timer clicked back together and powered down. The egg timer looked like it did when Seefer first took it out of the case.

The device incinerated everything inside its funnel of light. The only light in the room came from cindering papers still clinging to the wall. The glow was enough for Seefer to recognize the person who took him down – Pavo. He didn't look happy.

"What have you done?" Pavo asked in a very stern voice.

"I don't know. Sorry. It looked harmless enough." Seefer said.

Standing up, Pavo said, "I am not talking about the Gamma-cone, though you should not have touched it! I am talking about you coming back here. Have you gone mad?"

"I thought I could stop him," he admitted.

Pavo laughed. "Who? Korvus? You nearly had your head removed by the Gamma-cone. What made you think you could handle someone trained to use weapons like that?"

"I didn't think. I acted. I figured if I was able to stop him, then all of this would go away and…and I wouldn't have to."

Pavo toned down his aggression. "Young one, I admire your courage. You were brave in taking these matters into your own hands. You must realize, no matter what we do from this point on, your world has already changed. There is no magic wand that can return you to yesterday as if none of this happened. Like it or not, your time in this town and this school is over."

"But what if we take down Korvus?" Seefer asked. "Then there is no one to run from."

"Is that what you think? He is not the only one

looking for you? There are more. And if Korvus is stopped, the others will know exactly where to look. We have no choice but to run."

Seefer paused and thought about life on the run, where their only destination would be the place furthest from their last. As exciting as life without school sounded, he couldn't bear to leave his mother – even if it meant staying long enough to bring her on board.

"I'm not running. Not without my mother."

The Bilco door opened, allowing light to refill the cellar dwelling. Cassy popped her head into view. "Can I come down there *now*?"

Seefer and Pavo gave half-hearted nods.

Cassy descended the stairs. "Why not let me stay up there longer? I thought you were going to call me down when the device was secure?"

She got no response.

She continued, "Well Seef, I did not realize how big of a pain in my butt you would be to look after. Coming back to the scene of the crime? Not so smart! Can we get out of here now?"

"No!" Pavo looked inspired by a revelation.

"No?" she asked.

Pavo answered, "We are here. Escaping again will prove to be too risky. Maybe it was in the first place. Like you said, a missing child report is the last thing we need. I believe a fight is in order."

Seefer was excited by the thought. Cassy looked

confused.

She said to Pavo, "You said we need to get as far away from here as possible or they will find him."

"Chances are they already know he is here. The perimeter shield around the school is still active which means they are. They have not yet moved onto a new location."

Pavo walked over to the door which led to the basement corridor. He slammed it closed and locked the deadbolt with a key. He then picked up the egg timer and placed it back in its case. While in there, he removed another device that looked like a silvery shot-put.

Seefer showed interest. "Whoa. What is that? Another weapon of some kind? X-ray window maker? Levitator?"

"No," Pavo said shortly. He shook the contraption and a bright-as-day light emanated from it. "It is a light bulb." When Pavo freed it from his grasp, the orb stayed hovering in mid-air. Seefer was mildly disappointed, despite the hovering effect.

Pavo continued to take inventory of his tools. He discovered the bracelet was missing. "Gravity band?"

Seefer embarrassedly took it out of his pocket and showed him it. "Is that what you call this?"

Pavo responded, "Yes." He paused a moment before saying, "Keep it. You may need it more than me."

Cassy said, "Pavo, can we be realistic? Korvus has dozens working for him. How are the three of us going to stop him? I was not hinting at a battle before. I was suggesting we pick up his mother."

Pavo moved some objects from his case into the pouches of his janitor uniform, ignoring Cassy the whole time.

She made no secret of her exasperation. "You know, it is not polite to ignore me. I have gone along with your plans up until now, but I expect you to keep us better informed if you intend on changing those plans – especially, if you are dragging us into a fight."

Pavo closed his case and stowed it beneath some tools on his workbench. He turned to Cassy and said, "I am doing no such thing." He headed toward the stairs.

"What do you mean? You said we would have to fight them?" Cassy challenged.

"No, I said there would be a fight, but it is one that I will have. You must stay here and protect the boy."

"Hey! I can protect myself!" Seefer exclaimed.

"Yeah, see?" Cassy reinforced.

"Kids…" Pavo paused. Cassy and Seefer waited for him to change his mind. "The light shuts off every 10 minutes. Shaking it will reignite the bulb." He slammed the Bilco door shut. Cassy and Seefer then heard the sound of a metal chain dragging along the surface of the door followed by a click.

"He locked us down here!" Cassy yelled in

exasperation. She ran up the stairs and began pounding on the metal doors with closed fists. With every strike, the doors spread open enough to see a sliver of daylight, but it was evident they were trapped.

The caged rats freaked out from all the noise. The squeaking of their throats and scratching of their claws reached a deafening level. Each cloudy white eye illuminated in the ghostly white glow of Pavo's hovering bulb.

Seefer ran up and stopped her. "Cassy, quiet! Let's not attract the wrong type of attention."

"How are you okay with this?" she asked as she darted across the room to try the other door. "Your first instincts were right. That guy gives me the creeps. What if he is holding us down here in order to bring the others to us?" She pulled and twisted on the door lever to try and open it. She failed.

"Wouldn't he have done that already, Cass? He's had chances. I mean we are just a couple of kids."

"Speak for yourself, gravity boy!" Cassy said.

"Whoa! What did I do? Plus, we're back here because of me, not him. He could take us down in a second if he wanted to. Did you see the way he handled that mop earlier?"

"Yeah, I saw him. Something is not right," she said.

"What makes you think that?"

Cassy stopped frantically moving around for a moment. "Because I was sent here to protect you too,

Seefer."

It made sense and no sense all at the same time. Seefer thought it explained why Cassy all of sudden became super-soldier in the midst of today's events. Finally, he said, "Huh?"

Cassy explained, "Your mother sent *me*. Months ago. She knew exactly how and where to find you. If trouble were to ever roll into town – like it did today – it would be my job to get you out."

"Uh, you are actually twelve, right?"

"Fourteen actually," she said.

Seefer threw his hands in the air after hearing yet another blind-siding revelation. "Figures you would be. Any other secrets you're hiding?"

"I am your sister," she said.

"What?! Really?!" Seefer exclaimed. His eyes bulged out. His breathing grew heavy.

"No!" Cassy burst out in laughter. "Just kidding. I can still have a little fun, right?"

Seefer nodded while he was still trying to catch his breath.

Cassy returned to a more serious topic. "If Pavo was telling the truth, he would not have had to run a gamut of tests on you this morning to find his *Cepheus*. He would have known where to find you. I don't believe his intentions are pure."

"Unless…" Seefer started.

"Unless, what?"

"What if he didn't know where to find me, because the person who sent you *couldn't* tell him?" Seefer proposed.

Cassy scowled at him. "That is your mother, Seefer. You should not have such thoughts."

"So it's true, then. The story he told about my mother?" Seefer had trouble saying those words and not imagining his *real* mom at the same time. He felt like he was betraying the only mother he knew.

"The story of your biological mother is true. The story of how our timelines came to split is a scientific fact that we learned in training. Aside from those tales, I am unsure about the credibility of anything else Pavo said."

"I can't believe I'm not really an Elliot," he said. "But I guess I know now where my mom got the name 'Seefer' from. Feels so fake now. I don't even have a real father?" He held his hands to his head to stop his world from spinning.

Cassy, still scanning the room for a way out, picked her head up long enough to recognize Seefer's anxiety. "Seef, if you think too hard about it, you will go crazy."

"I'm waiting for the dream to be over. I'm going to wake up in my room and this will all be some crazy, goofy dream that I came up with," Seefer convinced himself.

"But you cannot get hurt in a dream without waking up," Cassy reminded him.

"So? When did I get hurt?"

Cassy took a swing and hit him in the arm.

"Owwww! You've got to stop doing that!" Seefer yelled as he clutched his upper arm in pain.

"Enough. Let us work on getting out of here." She looked up around the ceiling, following the pipes running across it.

Seefer wasn't ready to follow. "Cassy, can I ask? Why should I trust *you*? You are a completely different person today. Up until this morning you were just…just…Cassy. You know. Happy Cassy. You loved the world and school and having fun. Now you are this…this…" Cassy shot him a warning look but it didn't deter him from saying, "soldier. You're beating up bad guys, jumping out of windows, and you keep punching me, which really HURTS!"

A tear emerged in the corner of Cassy's eye.

Seefer felt bad for attacking her. "Cassy, I'm…"

"You had your say, Seef." She raised her hand to stop him from speaking further. She dug deep to confess some true feelings. "I do love this world of yours. I wish I could forget the reason I came here and blissfully live as a student at lowly Harrison Middle School, but I cannot. I am from a world where humans are not in control. Our Earth, my Earth, is a place of hostility and sadness. We live each day wondering if we will be captured or killed. We wonder if, asleep in our shelters at night, our thirst or hunger will be enough to keep us from seeing the next day. We wonder when our hope will return. In other words, life sucks there.

"But this world, though…is full of *great* wonder. And it is the simplicity of what you strive for that makes it *beautiful*. Art, music, and dance? That is alien to me. With knowledge and technology, our world grew very cold. Science has provided many goods, but it came at the expense of enjoying what makes us human.

"When the Gliesians arrived, they provided us with countless amounts of technology. Everything became scientific. If something did not serve to better the human race, it was eliminated. Museums, churches and theaters were abandoned. They were replaced by more libraries, more laboratories and more schools. The balance between the arts and sciences was lost.

"That was all before my time. I never knew of happier times, until I came here.

"The girl you know – or knew before today – was in awe of this world. My awe and appreciation are not feigned. My enthusiasm is real. I love everything here. From the music you play in your gasoline-powered vehicles to the little chocolates they give us in the cafeteria for dessert. These are things I never had. Being *human* felt good for a change." She welled up with tears. "But today, things got real. I had to get real, Seefer. I am doing the best I can at the one job that I was assigned to do – protecting you."

Seefer wasn't expecting to touch such a nerve with Cassy when he challenged her change of demeanor. After her pouring out of emotion, he started feeling uncomfortable.

To lighten the mood, Seefer said, "So you like art class, huh?"

The two of them laughed a bit for a much needed break in the tension. Cassy looked toward the ceiling and something caught her eye.

"Hey, Seef, do you think you can boost me up there?" she asked.

Seefer saw the open vent she was eyeing. It sat above the hallway exit. "Maybe," he said.

Cassy pushed Seefer's head down and directed him into a crouched position. Then she steadied herself behind his shoulder. "Stand," she said.

Seefer stood up. Cassy leapt off his shoulders and grasped onto the edge of the vent's opening. She didn't dangle for long before displaying an amazing surge of power that propelled her into the hole.

"How do you do that?" Seefer said as he marveled at Cassy.

She popped her head out and looked down at him to say, "A life of training." Then she disappeared into the shadows.

Seefer heard a thud on the other side of the door. Cassy landed safely.

"You okay, Cass?"

"I am alright!" she yelled.

"Nice! Now can you get me out of here?" Seefer asked.

"No," she replied matter-of-factly.

"What? Why?" he said.

"Remember, Seef. I am here to keep you safe. You stay there, and I will make that happen," she shouted through the wall.

"You're leaving me down here?"

After a short pause, Cassy responded, "Yeah. Sorry. I will return." He could hear her footsteps trail away.

Seefer felt very abandoned all of sudden. The only allies he had were suddenly gone, leaving him alone in the cold, dingy basement. Pavo's hovering light bulb was the sole source of warmth.

But at that instant, the light fizzled out leaving Seefer in a cold, dingy, *dark* basement. The only word that came to his mind was, "Freck."

14

With so many different yard and power tools lying around in pitch-black darkness, the janitor's workshop became a dangerous place to walk around in.

Seefer's eyes hadn't adjusted to the sudden loss of light. He fumbled over some objects close to the work bench, but managed to stay unharmed. The insidious sound of hungry and frightened rats echoed through the chamber. This actually helped Seefer keep his bearings. Knowing where the rats were crated, he situated himself relative to their sounds.

He made it to the middle of the room, or what he thought was the middle. "Where is that light?" he mumbled to himself.

Reaching his hands out in front of him, he felt warmth. As he inched forward, his hands grew warmer as he approached the still-hot orb.

"Ow!" he yelped. Seefer reached too close and touched the bulb. *How am I supposed to shake it if it's this hot?* Seefer quickly thought up an idea. He took off his shirt, wrapped it around the bulb and shook vigorously.

The orb reignited and cast its bright glow throughout the room again.

Seefer looked away for a moment so he could adjust to the sudden brightness. Once his eyes could tolerate the brightness, he searched for a way out.

"There's got to be a ladder around here somewhere," he said to himself. After searching for one, nothing turned up. There wasn't anything sturdy enough for him to use to get closer to that vent.

He then tried something he wished he thought of earlier. He stared at the door and allowed his sixth sense to overtake him.

Fixated on the door's lock, he tried to feel the mechanisms inside of it. Strain filled his face as he attempted to make it open. This was no napkin or newspaper. The door contained many complex and dense objects that would need to be moved in order to unlock it. Seefer concentrated deeply.

Ultimately, he failed and the door remained sealed and shut.

Frustrated, Seefer picked up a wrench from the ground and hurled it against the wall. Tools fell off hangers and onto the workbench. The loud racket, the clanging of metal on metal and the jingle of keys stirred the rats again and also could have attracted unwanted guests.

Wait...keys? Seefer looked again. It was, in fact, a

huge ring of keys. He wished he had looked a little harder before.

He grabbed the ring and pawed through the tens of keys looking for one that matched up with the deadbolt on the door. He tried out a few. Some fit but didn't engage. Some wouldn't even enter the slot.

After about twenty tries, he found the key that would unlock the door. Seefer pocketed the key ring for safe keeping. He opened the door, but before exiting, turned to the rats and said, "Hopefully, I won't be seeing you guys again."

Seefer found his way back up to the first floor. The daylight shining in through the classrooms was a welcome sight. Walking through the main corridor, he was not surprised by the absolute silence. As a trained soldier, Pavo was probably navigating the halls looking for bad guys at that very moment, like a ninja in the dark. Cassy displayed a few stealthy skills of her own. So unless they wanted to be seen, he wasn't going to find them.

Then he thought about why exactly he was roaming the halls in the first place. If he was caught out in the open, he would be forced to fight. Plus he was without his two best lines of protection. *Maybe leaving the basement wasn't such a good idea.*

He entered a nearby classroom, one with a view of the front lawn. When he neared the room's windows, something outside caught his attention – a school bus.

He looked up at the clock. *Already 3:15?* All of the buses would be arriving shortly. There was always one driver that arrived early and spent time reading the newspaper until dismissal. From what Seefer could tell, there was no driver on that bus. *Where is she? If she tries to enter the school she'll be knocked out like the cop was.*

"Oh no." Seefer looked over at the police cruiser. The bus driver, a woman dressed like she was about to do some gardening, crouched over and leaned into the car. She appeared to be trying to wake up Officer Booth.

When she stood up straight, Seefer could see she was on a cell phone.

"What is she doing? No, don't call anybody else!" With good reason, Seefer didn't want more people to get hurt.

Seefer opened the window and yelled out to her, "No! Don't call anyone! It's not safe!"

The bus driver looked up at Seefer whose head hung out the window with his arms waving wildly. She took a big dutiful breath and responded, "Right! Stay there. I'll get help!"

Then as fast as her old creaky legs could move her, she ran aboard her bus and drove off. Seefer yelled "Wait!" so he could explain further, but the lady was gone surprisingly quick.

Seefer came back into the room. "She *may* have misunderstood me just a tad."

He exhaled deeply while deciding his next move. His stomach growled and made the decision easy for him. Patting his belly, Seefer calmly said, "You're right. It's going to be a long night."

The running around had made him hungrier than normal. He decided that if a fight was what he was in for, he had better have a full stomach.

Seefer scoped out the cafeteria before entering. His first step made a loud squeak that echoed through the empty hall. He froze. *Did anyone hear that?* It appeared no one had. He took another step. His sneaker squeaked again.

Seefer looked down and saw that both of his feet were sloshing through a puddle of sticky juice that had spilled on the floor. The rubber soles of his sneakers were squeegeeing the liquid across the tile making his presence very noticeable. Looking at the mess, Seefer remarked, "They really need to get a new janitor."

To clear the puddle, he took a giant leap and landed over on clean flooring. The liquid on his shoe didn't allow him to plant properly, and he oafishly slipped into one of the dining tables.

Careful not yell, Seefer clutched his knee and upper arm and quietly squirmed. "Ow, ow, ow."

The pain subsided after a few seconds. He rose to his feet and continued walking.

With only steps to go before entering the kitchen, he heard a clatter come from inside. *Who could that be?*

The kitchen's swinging doors had square windows mid-way up them. Ever so cautiously, Seefer put his face close to one of the windows to catch a glimpse.

With one eye peering into the kitchen, his field of vision wasn't the best. He couldn't see anything. Even though he was anxious to find the source of the noise, he remained careful not to be too anxious and risk showing himself.

Seefer spotted something on the counter where the staff regularly prepares food. It looked like a helmet. *Drones are in there!* The helmet in Seefer's view had a giant shatter crack running down the front visor. That helmet belonged to his would-be kidnapper.

Seefer's heart raced. He knew the guy that belonged to that helmet wouldn't be too far away. He heard a noise. The door to the walk-in freezer opened. A cloud of cold air rushed into the kitchen, temporarily blocking Seefer's view.

When the cloud dissipated, he could make out a figure. He had his back turned toward the door as he was crouched over the counter. He looked like he was eating something.

Then he turned around and Seefer could see that a giant jar of grape jelly was stuck to his face. The drone lifted the jar in the air and started tapping the bottom. *He wasn't stuck. He was eating.*

It took only a few more seconds for him to finish off the jelly before lowering the jar. Seefer wasn't expecting what he saw next.

He – or it – wasn't human!

Seefer quivered as he looked this *thing* up and down. Even though it stood erect, its head was far from anything human. Seefer wasn't sure what it resembled. It had a long tubular grey snout, freckled with hair and moles. The snout bunched and extended as the creature slurped up the last of the jelly from its fingers. *Where are its eyes?* There were two small marble-sized beads above the snout. *Could those be them?*

Okay, I'm dreaming. Even though he believed parts of Pavo's story, there were still elements that seemed too unlikely to be true – namely, the part about the aliens. Now the proof was tearing up his school's kitchen!

Seefer watched as the creature cleaned off its feeding tube. The outer orifice peeled back, and several thin tentacles protruded outward to lick up the rest. "Disgusting!" Seefer muttered to himself.

In an instant, the creature stopped everything it was doing. The tentacles retracted back into its snout. The outer walls returned to their original shape. Then the creature's head began probing its surroundings.

Seefer realized he might have spoken too loudly. The creature was on alert sensing something was not right in its presence. It raised its snout in the air and exhaled loudly. The noise it produced came out sloppy and wet – like a messy sneeze. The sound was almost laughable. If it weren't for his shaking in fear, Seefer would have had a good belly laugh.

Seefer figured it would be a good time to get out of there. Just before he peeled his eye away from the window, he watched as the walk-in cooler door opened again. Two more drones emerged. With helmets in hand, the first one communicated with the others in that same sloppy, wet sound.

No more spying. Time to go. Seefer backed away from the door and bolted toward the cafeteria exit. On his way to the door, he failed to exhibit caution around the juice spill. His first step into the mess sent him skidding forward into the hallway ahead. He crashed into the front metal panel of the drinking fountain mounted on the opposing wall.

KKBLANG!

The crash was loud. Seefer picked himself up quickly. He knew anyone within a hundred meters would have heard that racket. When he rose to his feet, he looked back. All of his instincts were correct. His clumsiness alerted them of his whereabouts, for Seefer was standing before three very angry-looking alien monsters.

He raised his hand and gave a nervous wave. "Hi, fellas!"

The apparent leader, the one who Seefer first saw, snorted in response. His two companions returned the gesture with snorts of their own.

Seefer realized that this was it. This was the fight he said he wanted. His enemy stood before him and looked eager to attack.

The creatures approached with a predatory stance. Seefer braced himself for their impending strike, but then he did the most logical thing that probably anyone would do in that situation – RUN!

He hauled his butt down the hallway as fast as his legs could take him, never looking back. Adrenaline surged through his veins, allowing him to sprint faster than he ever had before. Any bump or bruise he incurred from his pair of falls didn't matter. He ran two hundred feet in what felt like five seconds.

Seefer needed to make it to the end of the corridor, where a pair of doors separated the hall from the main staircase. He put every ounce of effort into each step to bring him there faster. *Almost there!* He couldn't afford any mistakes now.

Within five feet of the doors, he leapt into the air. His legs led the way as he kicked in the push handle. His forward momentum swung the door open as he slid safely onto the landing atop the stairs. He quickly stood up and slammed the door shut. With one quick pull, he yanked his belt out from his pant loops. Feeding it through the pull handles on the door, he fastened the belt tight and stepped back to catch his breath.

Seefer breathed heavily. He had never run that fast for so long before. He actually couldn't believe he pulled off the escape without fainting or messing up badly. As he was gasping for air, he wondered why the creatures hadn't caught up yet.

Curiosity got the best of him. He inched forward

toward the doors. He had to look through the thin pane of glass to see where they were. When he got close enough to see, there was nothing.

"They didn't follow me?" Seefer asked himself.

BAM! The door jolted open and hit him in the nose. It started bleeding immediately. He crawled backwards and watched as the monsters tried to get in. They rapidly shook the door on its hinges, but couldn't break the belt to open the door.

"What?!" Seefer yelled with his arms raised, perhaps a tad cockily.

A heavy wheezing noise came from the creatures, like the activity was giving them some breathing problems. With the makeshift lock holding and the aliens sounding unwell, Seefer wasted no time getting further away. Ignoring his bleeding nose, he fled down the stairs. He paid no attention to the trail of blood he left in his wake.

As he descended the stairs, the sound of the rattling doors stayed a reminder to keep going – keep moving. He reached the bottom of the staircase and exited out onto the first floor. Before he continued down the hall, he remembered something.

"The keys!" he exclaimed. He reached into his pocket and pulled out the ring of keys he took from the janitor's room. He returned to the doors and closed them tight. He looked closely at the lock on the door and saw a code, *S002*.

It took a moment, but Seefer noticed similar codes

on all the keys he held. He flipped through ones that began with C, L, O, and then found S. There were four *S* keys on the ring. Then it made sense. There were four sets of staircases in Harrison Middle School.

He found the *S002* key, inserted into the lock and turned. At least this would add another obstacle for those drones to deal with if they should break through the belt.

Seefer stowed the keys and hobbled into a nearby bathroom. He only spent a few seconds inside before coming back out with a wad of toilet paper applied to his nose.

When he entered the foyer of the school, he closed the doors to the main corridor behind him and locked them. Beside that set of doors, stood a statue of President William Henry Harrison, for whom the school was named. Seefer wedged himself between the statue and the wall. With an effortful heave, he summoned enough strength to tip the statue over in front of the doors.

"Sorry, Willy," Seefer said with a heavy heart.

Time to get out of here! He looked back once to make sure he wasn't being followed. There was no sign of danger. He breathed a sigh of relief. Reapplying the wad of tissues to his face, he exited the building.

When he stepped outside, the unexpected sound of people and sirens filled the air. He questioned whether he was hearing things. When Seefer pulled the bloody napkins away from his face, he found that he wasn't imagining anything.

Police aligned the entire front border of the property, with every police cruiser in town parked alongside the road. Officers were setting up wooden barricades along the front sidewalk to prevent anyone from passing by. As buses pulled up to the school to pick up kids for dismissal, cops were waving at them to move along. A group of parents who arrived early to get their children were being herded away despite their insistence on entering the school.

The commotion ensued. As more cars pulled up to the school, the cops were running out of places to direct them. Every parent wanted answers as to why they weren't allowed to enter the school.

Someone must have noticed Seefer standing on the school steps, because a quiet trickled over the crowd as one by one they all turned toward the steps. Seefer stood before them as the center of attention covered in his own blood. A rush of embarrassment overcame him. He nervously waved to the onlookers.

A familiar face waved to him from the barricade – Officer Booth. *He's alright!* Seefer acknowledged him and moved down the steps.

On his way toward the road, Seefer looked back at the school to see if anyone was watching. He didn't see anything unusual. He moved forward.

"Seefer!" a voice cried out from the crowd.

"Mom?"

Seefer saw his mom corralled into a group with all

of the other parents. When she saw her son, she clipped and clawed her way to the front of the crowd.

"Are you okay, baby?!" she yelled.

"I'm alright!"

When she got close the barricades, a few officers tried to turn her around. They held their arms out so not to let her by. "Don't you dare!" she warned. "That's my son!"

She swiped away the cops' arms and ducked under a barricade. They tried to grab her, but she began running toward her son.

"No, Mom!" Seefer ran toward her. He held up his hands and waved frantically. "Stay there! Stay there! I'm coming!"

Booth saw Seefer's mom break through and realized the danger she was in. If she proceeded too far, she would be knocked out instantly like he had been. "Ma'am, stop right there!" He darted after her.

Seefer ran as fast he could, needing to make it through the shield first so his mother wouldn't run into it. He could see where it was – the grass on the front lawn was folded away along its crease. He couldn't muster up enough speed to beat her to that critical point. She was faster and would beat him there. "No mom! Listen! Stop!"

Only a few strides away from unknowingly running into the shield, Booth flew in from her blind side and tackled her to the ground.

She frantically tried to free herself as he sequestered her on the ground. Other cops ran toward them. She twisted and flailed trying to get out from under Booth. "Let go of me. I can't go after my own son?"

Seefer made it up to the edge of the shield. "Let her go!"

"Kid, do you want your mom to go home with a splitting headache? Cuz that's what I got!" Booth yelled over. "I don't know how you made it all the way through, but I don't want to see anyone else get hurt."

"Mom, listen to me!" Seefer got her attention. "You have to listen. If you come in here, you'll get seriously messed up. There is some type of force field here that can't be crossed. I saw this policeman get thrown back like twenty feet and knocked out cold."

She thought that was nonsense. "What are you talking about, Seef?"

"I can explain, but PLEASE believe me. If he lets go, stay there."

Mom looked at him and saw deep sincerity in his eyes. "Okay, I will."

"Now can you let her go?" Seefer pleaded to Booth.

Booth felt his mom relaxing beneath his restraint. "You agree to stay right here?" She nodded in agreement. "Okay then," he said as he released her. She stood up and sneered at Booth. He raised his hands in innocence. "Just trying to save your life. Sorry."

Seefer's mom talked to him. "What is going on in

there? Are you alright?"

"Yes. I'm okay."

"But you're bleeding!"

Seefer wiped his nose. The bleeding stopped, but blood had dried and streaked down his face. "It's nothing, Mom. I slammed my face in a door."

"Hey kid, where is everybody?" Booth interrupted. "Did you find anything in there?"

"Just trouble!" Seefer retorted.

Mom shot Booth a look. "Do you mind? I'm trying to have a conversation with my son."

Seefer shouted, "Mom, I'm okay. Everyone in the school is missing. We haven't been able to find them."

"We?" she asked.

Booth said, "The girl. Casey?"

"Cassy," Seefer corrected. "And the janitor."

"Oh, the janitor is on your side now? Thank goodness." Booth said.

"Honey, I know you want to help but look at you. Let these men do their job."

One of the other cops who gathered around motioned Seefer to come closer. "Yeah, kid. Let's get you safe."

Seefer acknowledged him but didn't follow the direction. It didn't feel right. Two minutes ago, he wanted nothing more than distancing himself from this school. He had faced an opposition that changed his mind about doing battle. He looked over at the crowd of concerned parents wondering what was happening to their children, and his mind began to change again. He couldn't leave. He was one of only three people that could help them. He had a duty to do something even if it meant getting a broken nose or worse.

He shook his head *no*.

"Seefer, honey, come on," his mom prodded. "Are you *able* to come out here?"

"Yes," he said. "I've crossed this line a bunch of times today."

"Then why?"

With a deep breath and a passing wave of courage, Seefer made his decision. "Mom, you said this morning that you want me to live up to my potential – to be more responsible. If I leave the school now, I won't be doing either."

"Honey, that's not what I meant."

"I know, but I think you might know how this is my responsibility." Dread took over his mother's face as she realized her son wasn't leaving yet. Seefer continued, "I have friends…er…classmates in there that need help."

Booth butted into the conversation, "But, that's why we're here, son," indicating the police presence.

Seefer looked around and saw a SWAT vehicle and more police cruisers pulling up to the school. "Yeah, but you're all out there." He backed up a step.

"Seefer! Come out here, please!" his mom pleaded.

Booth supported the sentiment. "Yeah kid. Don't be foolish. You'll be safer out here."

Seefer took another step back. "I'm sorry mom. I love you." Then he turned and ran back toward the school.

His mother tried to go after him, but the cops surrounding her had the good sense to hold her back. "Noooo! Seefer come back!" She fell to the ground crying hysterically.

Seefer reached the top of the stairs. He looked back at his mom before entering. She was torn apart, watching him with tears running down her face. Her pain made him think about whether he was doing the right thing going back in. Then Seefer did something very simple. He stopped over-thinking things and went inside.

In the foyer, everything looked the same as minutes earlier. The statue still blocked the door. Nothing appeared to follow him out of that hallway.

He climbed atop the statue so he could look through the windows on the doors. Everything seemed quiet. Something seemed *too* quiet about it all. Those creatures went after him with an aggressive pace. They obviously wanted to get him, but they stopped their pursuit.

Seefer decided the best thing to do is stay put and not go scouting as he did before. With the key labeled *G0003*, he locked the entrance to the gymnasium. Now only one door stayed open, the one to the main office.

He would camp there.

He sat down in one of the waiting chairs just inside the door, taking a load off his feet. He had sit in these chairs before, but never appreciated how soft and cushiony they were. He had been running around so much all day, that this moment of rest felt like the greatest gift he'd ever been given.

Daylight faded – sunset only a half hour away. Seefer usually would be bummed about this. He used to hate the clock falling back because it meant shortened playtime after school. On a day like today, a nap would make for the most ideal afternoon event. The chair he sat in was the only thing he needed.

His eyes grew heavier. Every blink he made, his eyes stayed shut a little longer. Then he blinked one last time before he kept them closed for good.

15

Seefer pushed the bad things out of his head. The noise from outside drifted away. Even loud police sirens sounded like calming white noise. All of the fearsome and anxious events of the day seemed like dreams themselves, as new thoughts of happier times flooded his mind.

Seefer reminisced about some of the funny things Cassy used to say or do prior to her *metamorphosis*. How she once ate an orange – rind and all – at lunch time. She was disgusted by the outer *shell*. When she was told that the *shell* was supposed to be removed, she grew eagerly excited for her next orange.

Seefer remembered Cassy's first music class. The instructor passed out instruments to be played that day. She was handed a clarinet. The long, dark woodwind piece studded with shiny knobs fascinated her, but she hadn't the foggiest idea how it worked. Seefer recognized her puzzlement and, with the clarinet he was holding, motioned to her that she should blow into it.

She did. A loud squelching noise emanated from it. She was thoroughly delighted even though it sounded like a duck dying. She only needed three classes before she kept pace with the clarinet players that had been learning since 3rd grade.

Seefer had regarded her little nuances as her being weird, but now he realized he was witnessing Cassy seeing and doing these things for the first time – like a toddler. She was innocent in so many ways. Yes, he saw a razor sharp edge of her today, but the other side of her was a delicate flower blooming in a new environment.

While Seefer dreamed about the positive things, his sleep deepened and his awareness faded. Even though he sat facing the lobby, he did not see the gymnasium door open.

Though he locked that door earlier, he didn't take care to block it off. Like all public buildings, any door leading toward an exit cannot be locked from the outside in case of an emergency. The bar handle on the inside was still cocked and ready to open if pushed. Someone was pushing it.

The door slowly opened and out stepped one of Korvus' minions. It was the one from the kitchen. It must have returned there because it was once again wearing its helmet, the one with the cracked lens. The suited creature did not look toward the office. The statue on the ground distracted it.

While it walked over to examine the statue, the gym

door gradually closed. With a gentle click and shake, it fully shut. The subtle noise stirred Seefer in the nearby office. He opened his eyes wearily, but something caught his eye. *Drone!*

He jolted upward but was careful not to make a sound. His heart raced as he surveyed the area. He knew he would have to do something fast, but quietly. He ducked down and stayed as close to the ground as possible, keeping a close eye on the action in the hall.

The drone cleared the statue out of the way, dragging the bronze likeness of Harrison by his head and sliding him to the side. Once the path was clear, it opened the doors. Two more drones entered ready to prowl.

I thought I locked those doors. Seefer didn't understand the concept of these one-directional locks, but he knew the office's door knob would lock from the inside if he could get there in time. He took no chances and quickly lunged for the door, slamming it shut and locking it at the same time.

The commotion immediately alarmed the drones. They hurried over to the door. Twisting the knob and clawing at the edge of the door, their attempts to enter failed. At this point, they hadn't seen Seefer. He took cover behind the administrative counter and didn't move. The creatures moved away from the door and looked through the windows next to it.

Sunset was near. The school still had no power, so sight was very limited. The majority of the light in the room came from search lights and the red and blue strobes on the police cars outside.

The drones were not content staying on the outside. They needed to inspect this dark office before them. One found a metal trash cylinder in the foyer. It heaved the barrel over its head and threw it against the window.

Luckily for Seefer, the glass was meshed with security wire. The glass pane spider-webbed but stayed in place. The drones tried to clear the glass to gain access to the room, but the underlying wires made it difficult.

Then one caught sight of something on the ceiling it took particular interest in. It communicated to its cohorts in their garbled language, instructing them on what to do next. Then like a snake shedding its skin, the drone removed its spacesuit.

It was covered in wrinkly grey skin. It no longer appeared to have the shape of a human. The suit acted as an exoskeleton for its natural, amorphous form.

The blob extended itself skyward, reaching for the ceiling tiles. Even though it grew by another four feet, it was still too short to reach the ceiling surface. The other two provided help, lifting the creature.

It pushed up one of the drop-ceiling tiles and slid it out of the way, then effortlessly inched its way into the area above. When the blob was out of sight, the other two walked near the office window. There they waited patiently.

Seefer peeked his head out from his hiding spot. He

saw the two mirrored faces scanning the office looking for any sign of life, but no longer trying to claw their way in. *Why are they watching? Where's the other one?*

Then a noise came from above. Seefer looked and wasn't quite sure what he was seeing. The ceiling appeared to move, like the drop tiles were swaying back and forth. He passed it off as an illusion made by the police lights outside. Then when he saw the two henchmen outside looking at the same thing, Seefer realized he was in for a visit.

One of the tiles shook and then disappeared behind the others. Out from the shadows, the creature's head emerged. It stretched out of the cavity and protruded toward the floor. Seefer marveled at the length of which its head extended. Two or three feet of head and neck crawled out of the ceiling before a section Seefer could only assume was its torso.

More of the creature's body slithered out. Now six feet of alien grossness hung from the ceiling. Seefer watched in amazement but could do little to stop it. Any movement he made would be seen by the other two. He held onto the chance the blob wouldn't find him.

The invader stretched out as far as it could before releasing its grip. Its body plopped onto the ground. As it toiled to regain some semblance of form, the two drones were tapping on the remains of the window and pointing toward the door. *It's going to let the others in!*

Seefer panicked. Dealing with one of these things was going to be difficult. He didn't want to tangle with three at once. He made a snap decision.

On the wall hung a commemorative aluminum bat signed by last year's baseball team (which went 15-0). Seefer quickly sprang up to dismount it from the wall. As soon as he came into view, the two drones outside went crazy pounding on the glass, trying to alert their cohort of his presence.

Seefer yanked the bat from the wall. Taking a firm grip on the handle, he ran to the main door of the office. With the greatest of might, he swung at the knob.

And missed.

The blob lying on the ground rose from the floor. It formed into a more humanoid shape.

"Holy chutes and ladders," Seefer said to himself. He didn't stare too long at his enemy. He needed to finish what he started. He held the bat up high and then swung it like a caveman club.

THWACK! The knob smashed to the ground.

Seefer had a brief moment of relief, cracking a smile for his marksmanship. The six-foot tall skin creature towering over him interrupted his moment.

Seefer acted quickly. He gripped the bat tightly and swung it upward where he thought the creature's face was. He connected, sending the top of the beast backward.

"Yeah, take that, Jell-O face!" Seefer taunted.

He celebrated too soon. The creature's head recoiled. Seefer took another swing. This time, a slithery limb stopped it in its path. Seefer tried to pull it back, but the monster ripped the bat away from Seefer's hands and threw it against the wall.

The monster stuck out its chest and hollered a battle cry. It looked down at the defenseless boy, and in its best attempt to mimic English speech, mouthed the words, "You. Come. With. Us."

"No!" Seefer responded matter-of-factly.

Irritated, the monster's mouth peeled back, opening wider and wider. The jellyfish-like tentacles started to show and wiggled out of its orifice. Teeth revealed themselves, as its head became one big gaping mouth.

"Oh yeah, that's going to convince me," Seefer wisecracked before he jumped quickly out of the creature's path. He dove behind the administrator's counter.

For a formless being, the blob moved with quickness that Seefer hadn't anticipated. Before Seefer could pick himself up from his dive, the creature was leaning over the counter, looking down on him.

Seefer flipped over onto his butt and crawled backwards, away from the monster. The creature and all of its disgustingness melted over the counter's edge and onto the floor. Seefer scurried faster away, taking a turn into the principal's office.

He bought himself enough time to rise to his feet. He closed his eyes and tried his very best to *sense* the creature with his gift. He couldn't. There was too much adrenaline coursing through his veins. The fear of what was coming around the corner was too much. He couldn't concentrate on anything else.

That thing he feared crept into the room. Seefer rose to his feet, but there was no place to go. He slowly backed away from the door until he bumped into the Principal Witik's bookcase. This was the end of the road.

"Would you consider not capturing me?" Seefer tried asking.

The monster responded with a series of snorts and grunts that resembled laughter. The *laughter* grew louder and more maniacal.

Seefer didn't appreciate being laughed at. He had enough of being ridiculed in school. No alien was going to come onto his turf and bully him around.

The lights flashed on! Then quickly went dark again. Seefer realized it was his doing. He was on edge and that affected some of the electronics around him. The distraction made the creature turn toward the light fixture. Seefer grabbed the nearest heavy object, a wooden plaque, and hurled it at the monster's head.

Like the bat, it annoyed the creature more than hurt it. Seefer didn't stop. He threw an academic trophy, an encyclopedia, and a bronze bust of Archimedes. The monster deflected each one. In the process, every object knocked it backward a little more.

Seefer used the space to move over to Witik's desk where he found more things to throw. He heaved a ceramic mug, but that missed and shattered on the wall.

He grabbed a picture of Principal Witik's family and flung it like a Frisbee. The picture broke on contact with the creature's skin. The shards of glass cut in. An orangey liquid oozed from the cuts.

The creature went berserk. It started swaying back and forth, knocking some art and teaching degrees off the wall. When it came to its senses, it roared at Seefer and paused to take some deep, heavy breaths before resuming its approach.

Seefer grabbed whatever he could and started throwing it: pens, notepads, a stapler and a paperweight. Nothing impeded the creature's advance. It climbed over the principal's desk. Seefer backed up against the window.

Towered over him, the creature growled in frustration. Seefer reached for the closest thing he could get his hands on, a half-drunk carton of milk, and tossed it into its mouth.

The alien blob flashed a look of terror as it spat and sputtered, freaking out that it had something in its mouth. Seefer couldn't believe that of all the things he had thrown, the principal's leftover milk was what had the most effect.

The creature was getting more irritated. It started gasping for air and wheezing for its breaths. It backed off the desk and stepped back against the wall to prop itself up. Then it swirled its head around while wailing in agony.

Seefer froze. The compassionate side of him felt

bad for what he had done. He debated helping it out, but quickly dismissed the thought.

The creature convulsed and its skin literally crawled. Allergic reactions bubbled and wormed all over its body. Its wallowing grew louder. Then with a moment of peace, it turned its sad beady eyes toward Seefer. Their eyes connected. Seefer saw its agony and felt terrible for causing it.

"Sorry," he said sincerely.

SPLURSH!

The creature exploded. Disgusting, smelly, milky orange liquid shot across the entire office. Not an inch was left uncovered. The gelatinous substance dripped from the ceiling and oozed down the walls.

Seefer was close to tears. He no longer felt guilt or grief, but gagged from the creature's insides covering him from head to toe. The texture felt like yogurt, except with a sandy grit mixed into it. And the smell! It reeked of something worse than salmon in a microwave. Seefer gagged when some dribbled into his mouth.

He had to get out of the office. The smell was unbearable. He took steps toward the door. Each one made a loud sloshing noise, but there was no avoiding it. The entire floor was covered in the goo.

When he finally made it to the doorway, he looked at the window into the hall. The other two creatures peered in for confirmation on what transpired. When they saw Seefer emerge, they knew their ally must have been defeated.

With no light other than the red and blue strobes from outside, visibility was difficult. Seefer could still see one of the remaining two drones shedding its spacesuit. Like before, the other provided a boost into the ceiling. Seefer knew he was going to get more company.

He looked back and saw no sign of any more milk. He would have to fight this one differently. *How?*

The dark blob crawled out of the ceiling like the first one. The one in the spacesuit watched from the hallway.

As the blob gathered itself and rose from the floor, Seefer made a mess of the secretary's desk, looking for anything he could use as a weapon. Too dark to use his eyes, his hands found something of decent weight, the external speakers on her computer. He ripped them off the desk and got ready to throw them.

The monster stood tall above Seefer. "Come!" it bellowed.

"What? I can't hear you!" Seefer hurled one of the speakers at its face. "Better turn up the volume!" Unlike the last one, the monster didn't flinch.

The monster roared with irritation. "No. More. Games!" it garbled.

"You're a much better *speaker* than your friend." He laughed to himself for making a stupid pun.

The monster sprung to attack Seefer. In that very

instant a brilliant white light illuminated the room. Neither the monster nor Seefer could see. Seefer could make out the sound of glass shattering coming from the hallway's direction.

"Boy! Move out of the way!" shouted a familiar voice. *Pavo!*

Seefer jumped to his side. He heard the sound of the blobby beast breaking pieces of furniture around the office. It was destroying everything in hopes to get him.

Seefer continuously rubbed his eyes in hopes they would adjust to the brightness in the room. He tried opening his lids, but it was still too bright.

"Roll to your left!" Pavo shouted.

Seefer obeyed. He heard the smashing of one of the waiting chairs off to his side. He opened his eyes. Even though it was too bright for comfort, he kept them open. He cringed through the pain.

He saw the hovering light orb near the ceiling. Pavo must have thrown it through the break in the glass. He looked quickly out in the hall and saw Pavo tangled in battle with the space-suited drone.

Pavo handled his affairs, but kept tabs on Seefer at the same time. He saw Seefer wasn't paying attention to his own problems. "Do not look out here! Behind you!"

Seefer dodged out of the way of the creature's advance, sending it head first into the security glass. Some chunks of the glass fell out, but for the most part, it stayed intact.

"Lure him out here!" Pavo yelled, as he emptied out a fire extinguisher on his opponent's helmet. The blinded enemy did not see the roundhouse kick Pavo delivered square to its face.

"I can't!" Seefer yelled. "I knocked the knob off the door!"

Pavo looked befuddled. "Why did you do that?"

"I don't know. Seemed like a good idea!" Seefer should have kept silent. The light-blinded alien was able to find him by the sound of his voice. When Seefer turned his attention back to the room, it was too late. The monster took a swipe, knocking Seefer against the wall.

"Uggghh!" Seefer grunted. "I thought you things wanted me alive?"

As Seefer gathered his bearings, the creature approached for more. "My. Comrade. Is dead. From you."

Seefer looked down and saw the remains of the other. The milky orange goo was all that was left of it.

"You will," the monster breathed in deep before shouting, "comply!" Its mouth opened wide and blew out a most unpleasant smell. Seefer acted fast. He climbed onto the seat of the nearest chair and dived headfirst into the monster's mouth. The creature got a surprising throat full.

Pavo finished off his opponent while there was a moment of distraction. He body slammed the drone into the ground leaving it motionless. Pavo then lifted back the mirrored plate and inserted one of his egg-timer devices.

He walked away from the body. A blue light shined inside the creature's helmet and then a splash was heard. The mirrored helmet prevented any of the deadly light from escaping.

The remaining creature laughed as Pavo approached the shattered window. Its amorphous smile projected an attitude that said, *that was easy.*

But Pavo saw something to his liking. An allergic hive developed on the skin of the blob. Then another. The creature's disgusting smile faded as it realized something was wrong.

Pavo's stern demeanor cracked for a moment and a hint of levity broke through. He smiled at the alien and quipped, "Something wrong?"

SPLURSHHH!

The creature erupted into a pile of goo. Its body dissolved into gelatin and splattered across the entire office. The explosion of guts revealed Seefer, who hung in the air for a split second, before falling to the floor. Covered in more milky orange jelly, he struggled to clear his mouth for air. When he clawed enough away, he let in a giant breath.

"Oh God! Oh God! It smells so bad. Smells SO bad!" he cried.

Looking through the broken area of the window (the only section of glass that wasn't covered in slime), Pavo showed his relief. "Good work, young one!"

Seefer was in no mood for congratulations. The smell and taste of the slime was about to induce vomiting. He couldn't get up. He was stuck to the congealing remains. "Please. Help me out of here."

"You have my keys?" Pavo demanded.

Seefer reached into his pocket and pulled out the keys, along with a ball of ooze. He tossed them through the broken section of the window pane.

Pavo used the slimy keys to enter into the main office. The opening of the door squeegeed a layer of coagulating gunk out of the way. Even though he had battled these creatures before, Pavo still cringed at the odor in the room.

"Oh my, it smells very bad in here," he said.

"You think?" Seefer said.

Pavo reached out his hand and pried Seefer from the sticky floor. He propped him to his feet. After Seefer was freely standing, Pavo quickly reached into his pocket and cleaned the gunk off his hands.

"Oh, did I get some on you?" Seefer said sarcastically.

"Yes, a little. No matter. I took care of it." Pavo responded, not picking up the sarcasm. "That was very impressive. Taking down two glokes like that is not easy."

"Glokes?"

"That is the common Earth name for that species, yes," Pavo said.

"Yes, well, it would have been nice to know they had severe allergy to milk!" Seefer expressed.

"Yes, and it also would have been nice if you had stayed safely locked away downstairs." Seefer hung his gooey head. Pavo quickly checked his scolding tone with a compliment. "But, if you had not shown the initiative to get out and fight, I would not have recognized the fearless brave I can call my ally."

Seefer appreciated the consideration as Pavo's ally. "Thanks. Now can we do something about this crud all over me?"

"I know where we can go," Pavo said as he left the door.

Seefer took one last look around the room. It was destroyed. The tables, desks, chairs, and walls were wrecked by the glokes' rampage. Everything else was ruined by the slime.

Something caught his eye on the way out the door. On the wall hung the poster that read "Milk: Be Mighty." Seefer chuckled and flexed his muscles.

"Be Mighty!" he cracked.

With lifted optimism he dashed out the door to catch up with Pavo.

16

Light steam filled the boy's locker room. The hovering light orb provided an eerie glow through the fog. Pavo stood outside of the showers with a folded towel and two bars of soap.

"More! I need more!" cried Seefer from inside the shower. His hand reached out with his palm held open. Pavo placed a bar of soap in it.

"I only have one more after this one!" Pavo reminded.

"The water is starting to get way too cold!" Seefer said with a shiver in his voice.

"Just keep scrubbing," Pavo asserted.

"The goo keeps getting stuck *on* the soap! How is that even possible? Nothing sticks to soap."

"This does. I am all too familiar with it."

Seefer called out, "More soap, please! Hurry. I don't know if I can stand this water any longer."

"Alright, that's enough. Shut it down," Pavo instructed. "If we are going to do this correctly, we will likely need showers later anyway," Pavo said.

"Finally!" The shower turned off. Seefer's feet slapped against the wet tile as he walked out. He held his arm out so Pavo could give him a dry towel. Seefer wrapped himself up and stepped down into the locker room. He sat down on a bench and began to shiver.

"Cold!" he exalted.

"No power, no heat." Pavo said. "You were lucky there was some warm water left in the tank when you began."

"Now what? I can't put my clothes back on." Seefer was hugging himself, rubbing his arms up and down trying to stay warm.

Pavo tossed him another towel. "Follow me."

The pair walked through the boys' locker room, as the glowing orb followed behind. They headed toward Coach Wilhelm's office. His office was situated at the end of a long row of lockers. The glass windows that separated his room from the changing area were always covered up by blinds.

Seefer found Coach's tendency to leave his blinds closed highly annoying. While no one wants their middle school coach watching them change, many boys took this privacy as an opportunity to torture the weak.

All too often, the class would be out of control by the time Coach intervened. As a result, Seefer became well-acquainted with the insides of these lockers.

When they entered the Coach's office, the first

thing Seefer did was open the blinds.

"Good idea. Always be watching," Pavo advised. He took out his key chain on his way to the door in the room's corner. Seefer had never seen that door opened before. He always assumed it was a coat closet or something mundane. The door itself was unlabeled, unassuming, and tucked away. There was no reason to think much more of it.

Pavo pulled the key for the door and slipped it into the knob. Anticipation filled Seefer as Pavo turned the knob. He entered into the pitch black shadows. When the orb followed Pavo into the room, it slowly shed light on everything inside.

Seefer's jaw dropped as he walked behind the orb. On his immediate right were stacks of sporting equipment: helmets for baseball and football, bats, boxes of uniforms, net-bags filled with soccer gear and an array of things Seefer wasn't even sure about. Gutter-style rails on the wall to his left housed the hundreds of different balls stored in the room. Basketballs, volleyballs, soccer balls and footballs lined the wall.

Seefer had little interest in sports and sporting goods, but the metal cabinet on the far wall made his eyes widen and his mouth water.

The cabinet had a vented front, not unlike a locker. Through the holes Seefer could see mp3 players, super-soakers, action figures, cell phones, and other things that students weren't allowed to bring to school.

"Contraband!" he grinned with amazement. "Why is all of this stuff back here?"

"I am not sure. Perhaps it is the only place they have room for it," Pavo said as he dug through a cardboard box. "What size are you? Medium? Large?"

"Small," Seefer said embarrassedly.

Pavo pulled out a fresh T-shirt and pants from the box and tossed it over to Seefer. The T-shirt was the standard grey school-issued gym shirt that all the kids wear in Phys. Ed. The pants were track suit bottoms in the bright orange school color.

"Got any underwear in there?" Seefer asked.

Pavo looked in the box next to it and pulled out a jock strap. He held it up as an offering.

"I think I'll pass." Seefer slipped the pants on underneath his towel and wore the T-shirt. Pavo threw him a ball of long grey socks to wear.

"Shoe size?" Pavo asked.

"Three."

Pavo sighed. "You need a growth spurt." Pavo looked through an entire bin of sneakers. The old shoes were collected from cleaned out lockers or old team-issued pairs that no one kept at season's end. "Finally!" Pavo pulled out a pair of aqua-colored turf shoes.

"Those are girls' sneakers."

"They are also the only shoe that will fit you," Pavo assured. "Put them on."

After Seefer laced up the sneakers, Pavo tossed him

a familiar device. "The gravity band," Seefer said aloud.

"You left it in your slimed pants," Pavo told him.

"How does this thing work anyway?" Seefer asked.

Pavo demonstrated with his hand. "When wearing it, making a fist will draw you toward anything your arm is pointed at. Relaxing your hand will free the attraction. If you want to repel, face your palm in the direction, but bend your knuckles."

"Can I try it now?"

"No, put it in your pocket."

Like a kid having a toy taken away from him, Seefer sighed in disappointment, but obliged. "Hey, I had some other stuff too."

"Nothing else you need." Pavo said. He found Seefer a sweatshirt to wear and offered it to him. "Alright. We are now ready. Let us keep moving."

Pavo turned to leave the room. "Wait!" Seefer stopped him. "Don't you think we should see what we can use in that cabinet?" He pointed at the confiscated goods.

"Toys and weapons of mischief?" Pavo asked. "I think we should stick to the highly advanced tools that I brought with me."

"Right there. In the very front. I see a super-soaker. In the very least, we should grab that." Seefer contested.

"What good would getting in a water fight do for

us?"

"Fill it with milk!" Seefer proposed.

Pavo looked impressed by the thought. "Not a bad idea, young one."

Pavo fished for the key that would unlock the cabinet. When he threw open the doors, Seefer nearly fainted at the sight of all the gadgetry. Besides the stuff he saw through the vent holes, there were spy gear, lighters, pocket knives, inappropriate T-shirts, cases of bubble gum, and a stack of fifty or so comic books.

"Whoaaaa!" Seefer pulled an issue from the stack and started thumbing through the pages. Pavo ripped it from his hands.

"That is not going to help us find or stop Korvus," Pavo reminded him. He grabbed the super-soaker from the top-shelf and put it in Seefer's arms. Seefer continued to scan the shelves. "Is there anything else you see?"

"Are those night-vision goggles?" Seefer asked.

Pavo looked at the headgear with green lenses in the front but wasn't sure himself. "You would know better than I would."

"Oh that's right. You have way awesome devices. You probably have contact lenses that do the job."

"As a matter of fact, I do," Pavo said.

"Well, I'll work with these." Seefer said, grabbing the set. "Also this, this and these." He took the pocket-knife, a lighter, and a handful of smoke bombs.

"Exhibit caution with those items." Pavo warned.

"I'm up against blob monsters from not only another planet but entirely different dimension. I think I can handle a few smoke bombs."

After grabbing a baseball equipment bag, which he armed with an aluminum Easton bat, Seefer packed up all of his items and followed Pavo out the door.

Pavo, carrying a baseball bat of his own, led him to the cafeteria. They entered with caution. Pavo saw the collapsed lunch table and dented water fountain. Seefer nervously looked around.

"Those glokes sure made a mess, huh?" Seefer suggested.

"Yes, not bad for creatures with size 3 feet." Pavo slyly responded. He stood above a very clear footprint of a size 3 sneaker that was left in a sticky juice spill.

Seefer embarrassedly laughed.

They walked into the kitchen and witnessed a major mess. Jars of sticky substances such as grape jelly and maple syrup were lying on the ground. Their contents were removed, probably eaten by the glokes.

"They like sugar." Pavo stated.

"I guess so." Seefer looked around in amazement. "But what's the deal with the milk? Why do they explode?"

"Most Gliesian species have demonstrated an allergy to milk, specifically from the hormones used on the cows that produce it. Not that there are many things that species from another planet should be eating on an alien world, but this was particularly bad. Glokes had the worst reaction to it by far. You have seen it. Because they have no skeleton, the muscles in their bodies are constantly working to maintain shape. That is like the equivalent of you or I sprinting relentlessly. When the allergen enters their body, it causes an extreme anaphylaxis that results in explosion."

"I don't know what half of what you said means."

"Then you should read more."

Seefer scoffed as Pavo entered the cooler and pulled out a gallon of milk. He uncapped the gallon and took a swig.

"Ah, I remember when milk tasted this good," Pavo said.

"It doesn't anymore?" Seefer asked.

"As part of our partnership with the Gliesians, humans agreed to eliminate foods that that were harmful to our visitors, which mostly meant dairy products."

"Your world has no ice cream?"

"I am not familiar with it. I have seen it here, but there is none to be found at home," Pavo explained as he packed the equipment bag with cartons of milk.

"Horrible! So why didn't they avoid eating and drinking these things?" Seefer asked exasperatedly.

"Seems like common sense, I know. I am sure it was a way for them to take away one of our natural weapons against them. They used our compassion against us."

"Well, whatever happened there, it's cool now because we've got tons of milk here," Seefer reassured.

"Yes we do," Pavo acknowledged.

They began filling up the super soaker and some more portable containers from the gallon of milk.

"You said the glokes have the worst reaction to the milk," Seefer started. "What other things are there?"

"Glokes are intelligent, but they are not the prime species from Gliese. They share their planet with other higher life forms, unlike here on Earth. One group, that we humans call the *Sentinels*, are more intelligent and take on the role of protector or leader for their planet. There were other beings that came with them to Earth: gigaverms, tillsnips, and nilpedes. Those, the nilpedes, you might be familiar with."

"How?"

"They were inside the rats I had sniff you out."

"Huh?"

Pavo explained, "The nilpede is a small parasite that burrows into a host's head. It has the ability to utilize all of the senses of the host animal while controlling motor skills and behavior."

"Like a puppeteer?"

"Exactly. The great thing is they are highly obedient to their master. I had a specific scent they needed to find. They were able to find you for me."

"And then you fed them cheese?" Seefer said terrified. "To kill them?"

Pavo unfazed, answered, "Of course. Their purpose was fulfilled. I could not let anyone else find out about them. I actually only used them when I was certain I was close. No sense letting rats loose and causing hysteria."

Seefer was unsettled. "I wish I didn't know that. I gave them a piece of that cheese."

Pavo saw the troubled emotions on Seefer's face. "Do not fret, young one. You had a soldier's edge when you jumped down the throat of that gloke. Remember, they are all against us – all part of doing battle."

"What about the rats?" Seefer asked.

"Oh, yes, I suppose the rats are collateral damage." Pavo exited the kitchen.

Seefer followed behind him. They crossed the cafeteria to look out the windows.

The windows overlooked the back of the Harrison Middle School property. All of the athletic fields were within view.

Pavo noted, "The perimeter shield can only be supported from within. That means its source of power is somewhere on this property."

"I wandered around this entire building, and besides the glokes I keep running into, there's no sign of anyone else," Seefer said.

"Right. So how do you hide four hundred people

without a trace of their whereabouts?"

"Magic?"

"There is no magic, young one, only science. The only way I know how to hide something in the broad moonlight is with an optimask."

"Optimist? Like being positive?" said a puzzled Seefer.

"No, *opti* as in *visual* and *mask* as in concealing something. The technology has been far from perfect and rarely used because of its flaws. The technology creates a tent or dome around an area and makes whatever is under it invisible. The Gliesians had the technology, but it was clumsy. It was designed for space travel, to be unseen when approaching a planet. However, when applied to terrestrial environments, it cannot handle complicated scenery like trees, grass and clouds."

"Cool."

"If they improved that technology, it is very possible we are looking out at them right now. We need a way to locate them without wandering around those athletic fields like sitting ducks."

Seefer took out his night vision goggles and scanned the back lot. He tried to find any clue that would signal Korvus' whereabouts. All he could see were the baseball and football fields as they normally were, except in the goggles' green hue.

"Those will not be any use," Pavo said. "Those goggles are picking up trace amounts of infrared, which is another form of light. The optimask would refract those waves as well."

"Bummer." Seefer continued to scan around. He looked closer to the building. Near one of the classroom wings, he saw movement. "Wait a second."

"What do you see?" Pavo asked.

Seefer continued to look in that direction. The building's edge stood out from the pavement surrounding it. It had an olive color to it. He knew he saw something down there. He kept looking. And then, a head popped out from around the corner. Through the goggles, the human head appeared as a very bright green, almost white figure. As the lens adjusted, Seefer could distinguish the person.

"It's Cassy!"

"Where?" Pavo asked.

"Down there, near the East wing staircase." Seefer pointed.

Pavo opened a tiny container and delicately lifted its content into his eye. Squinting the other, he peered out the window using his night vision contact lens. "You two do not know how to follow orders. Where is she going?"

"I don't know. She took off on me without a word to what she was doing." Seefer said.

Pavo sighed. "I suppose we should go retrieve her before she makes trouble for us or herself."

"I think that might be too late," Seefer said.

"Why?"

Seefer watched Cassy turn the corner and enter the East wing's staircase. Not too far behind her were three glimmering figures. The goggles adjusted to reveal – "Glokes! Three of them are following her!"

17

Seefer and Pavo raced down the corridors to intercept Cassy. Pavo moved fast while traveling efficiently light. Seefer struggled to keep up. The extra stuff he carried in his backpack compounded his typical oafishness. The night vision goggles bobbled around his head as he ran.

"Quickly!" Pavo shouted.

"I'm trying!" Seefer shouted back.

Pavo burst through a staircase entrance and descended the steps as if he glided on the air above them. Seefer meticulously watched each stair as he covered them one by one.

They made it to the first floor. They hurried down the hallway and banked left into the east wing. Pavo then stopped. Seefer pulled up his sprint. His new turf shoes were screeching along the tile floor. He had to bump into Pavo to come to a complete stop.

"What gives?" Seefer asked.

"Silence," Pavo demanded.

They both stared down the empty hallway. Seefer didn't understand why he needed to be silent. "I don't see anything," Seefer said.

Pavo sniffed the air. He looked to the side, above and all around. "They are all around us."

Seefer tried to follow Pavo's eyes, but the goggles made it difficult to turn his head quickly. Every jerk of the head caused him to steady the device and allow it to focus.

"I don't see anything!" Seefer said with a hushed tone.

Pavo grabbed the top of his head and pointed him toward the end of the hallway. Seefer's goggles adjusted to the change of scenery. When the blackness faded and the green light was absorbed, he saw a drone running right for them.

He gripped his super-soaker tightly, aiming forward. Pavo put his hand over the gun and pushed it down. He whispered, "Save it until its suit is off."

Then what can be used now? Seefer lowered the milk-filled gun and readied his grip on the 31-ounce Easton on his back. *Oh, yeah!*

The drone closed in. Thirty paces. Twenty. Ten. It leapt into the air, and lunged toward Pavo and Seefer. *CRACK!* Pavo put it down with a swing of his bat. The mirrored face of the gloke's helmet shattered into a thousand shiny pieces.

"Yeah!" Seefer shouted in exuberance. "Nice one, Pavo."

With the gloke's face revealed and hanging out of its exoskeleton suit, Seefer recognized the opportunity to put it away.

"Now?" he asked.

"Now." Pavo signaled.

Seefer let go of the bat and aimed his milk-filled super-soaker directly at the gloke's mouth, but did not fire. The gloke quivered. It reeled in pain from the impact of Pavo's hit. Through his night vision goggles, Seefer could see fear in this particular creature's eyes.

"I–"

Pavo acted quickly and pulled the trigger on the super-soaker for Seefer. "No! What are you doing?" Seefer exclaimed. A powerful spray of milk shot into the gloke's mouth. More went down the cavernous throat of the creature than it could hope to spit out. Its eyes grew with concern as it knew what would happen.

"Saving your life, if you have not forgotten!" Pavo responded. He pulled his arm around Seefer and ran for cover. Seefer looked behind as Pavo dragged him from the gloke. He could see it trying its best to spit all the milk from its cavity.

The effort wasn't enough. The milk began reacting. Bubbles appeared on the skin surface, and agitation grew throughout. With one last gasp the gloke exploded. *SPLURSH!*

Unlike the last two kills that Seefer witnessed, this one was much more contained. The suit it wore shielded the hallway walls from a gooey blast. Only this

186

gloke's head debris made a mess in the direction it was pointing toward – the ceiling.

"Never hesitate!" Pavo asserted.

"It looked like it was going to say something." Seefer responded.

"There is nothing a gloke has to say that is worth your while. If roles were reversed, it would have killed you instantly," Pavo said.

Seefer thought about it for a moment and what Pavo was saying wasn't wholly accurate. "Roles have been reversed, and I am still in one piece."

"Only because they need something from you."

"So does that mean everyone who went missing is dead?" Seefer asked.

Pavo abruptly stated, "If we do not succeed and you get captured, then yes, probably."

Seefer stopped asking any further questions. He had plenty to ask, but didn't trust any answer he would receive. There was something that wasn't adding up in his head. The Gliesians wanted Seefer for their survival. And it would make sense to not harm anyone who is being held captive. For all of the schools they may have scoured before, their biggest advantage was discretion. If any student at those schools went home with a bump or bruise, a full-scale investigation would occur as to how that happened. Eventually, evidence would lead back to Korvus.

Maybe it would have been better to flee. The guilt

grew inside of Seefer. If he had sucked up his fears of being on the run, Korvus would not have found what he was looking for. Everyone would be released as if nothing had happened, but he selfishly returned to stop Korvus. If he were discovered, then everyone might be in danger.

Seefer weighed all of these thoughts in seconds as if the entire day flashed through his mind in a blur. He forgot for a moment that he was in the dark and surrounded.

"Gloke! To your left!" Pavo shouted.

Seefer raised the bat high and took a tomahawk chop down on the gloke's helmet. He could not duplicate the same amount of force as Pavo, though, and the strike hardly damaged the visor.

Pavo dashed over and prepared to strike. When he cocked back his bat, something grabbed him from behind. Pavo turned and saw a naked gloke staring him in the face. The large head dwarfed Pavo's. When it opened its mouth, it easily could have swallowed him whole. It inhaled before letting out a huge roar. The smell that came from within disgusted Pavo, but he kept his composure.

He released his grip on the bat the creature held, and the gloke jerked back an inch. With that slight disruption in balance, Pavo struck it in its tiny eye with his closed fist. The creature reeled in pain.

"I could use that milk," Pavo suggested.

Seefer was in the midst of his entanglement. The

gloke he faced moved significantly slower when stuffed inside its spacesuit. Seefer took advantage by making quick sprints and jukes to avoid it. He removed his backpack and set the super-soaker down to improve his speed. The attacker made attempts to bear hug him, but Seefer nimbly avoided them.

In the moments the gloke opened its arms, Seefer jabbed the bat into its face or chest. He wanted one lucky hit to break or tear the costume, but his attempts were ineffective.

He heard Pavo shout out for milk. "It's over there!" Seefer said pointing to a pile he made under a fire extinguisher.

"Best not to voluntarily give up your weapons when facing an enemy!" Pavo yelled while delivering another blow to the gloke's other eye.

Seefer started, "I-"

"Never mind!" Pavo cut in. The gloke opened up its weakness twice; it was not going to make the same mistake again. The blob started to morph its shape so it was wider and taller, as if it was using its body to separate Pavo from Seefer.

Before the blobby mass could completely close him off from Seefer, Pavo ran perpendicular to the hall, propelled himself up the lockers, and grabbed onto one of the ceiling pipes. With a thrusting swing he threw himself over the gloke and onto the other side.

When he landed, Pavo saw Seefer still going at it with his opponent. Seefer held his own, but not making any advances.

"Use the gravity band!" Pavo instructed.

Seefer's eyes lit up. He completely forgot he had it with him. He took a few big swings to fend off the gloke long enough to slip his hand into his pocket. When he pulled his hand out, the band encircled his wrist.

Seefer raised his hand, palms open, like someone about to deliver a karate chop. He smiled and said with a grin, "Let's get ready to rumble."

The gloke shook its head, but Seefer didn't take the suggestion. He slowly closed his fist. At the moment his four fingers touched his palm, he shot forward like a ball from a cannon.

His hand pulled the rest of his body forward like it was attached to a rocket. With a powerful impact, he smashed the drone's visor into pieces, sending it to the ground. Seefer relaxed his fist, stopping his forward momentum.

"Aggghhh!" Seefer cried. "That hurt!" He clenched his teeth and wiggled his fingers loosely. Despite the technology that drove his fist flying across the corridor, there was little to protect his skin and bones from the impact.

Pavo's opponent shifted shapes again and turned its head over the wall it built from its body. The large mass fully extended to the ceiling, dwarfing Seefer and Pavo.

As the two watched the wall of wrinkling flesh tower above them, the gloke Seefer took down was slithering out of its suit. Seefer and Pavo backed away from the first one, but didn't notice the second expanding and blocking off the other direction between the humans and their bag of weapons.

The fully expanded creature encroached on Pavo and Seefer. Pavo tried to protect Seefer by nudging him behind and staying in front. When Seefer turned to watch his step, he saw more trouble coming.

"Uh, Pavo," he said. "We have a bit of problem."

Pavo looked behind and saw the second gloke rising to the ceiling. They were trapped. To their front and rear were humongous masses of alien blob. To the right and left there were only lockers. They had nowhere to go. There was a span of only forty feet between the two monsters; and it was shrinking fast. The more time wasted, the less room they would have to maneuver.

"This is why you never part with your weapon, young one," Pavo said.

"Noted," Seefer replied. The forty-foot area quickly shrank to thirty. Seefer felt more claustrophobic than ever. "We're about to become a sandwich. A really, really gross sandwich!"

They looked in opposite directions ensuring no sudden moves were made from the imposing monsters. An idea popped into Pavo's head. "You are still wearing the gravity band, yes?"

"Yes."

"You will have to use it again – the same way as before. This time, be relentless. You have to rattle them enough so we can escape," Pavo commanded. "But young one, avoid their mouths. We have nothing to get you out at the moment."

Seefer liked the plan, despite the tender knuckles from his last strike. "When?" he asked.

With the constantly shrinking floor space, Pavo looked surprised he had to answer that question. "Any time would be good," he said.

Seefer aimed the banded wrist toward the gloke in front of him. He softly closed his fist. "Here we go."

FWOOSH!

He sprung forward and buried his fist into the eye of the gloke before him. The gloke was highly irritated and squealed from the impact. Seefer spread his fingers, shutting down the gravity band.

"Again!" Pavo shouted.

Still suspended in the air, Seefer pointed his arm toward the other gloke. He clenched his fist and flew across the open space. His body zoomed forward and shot straight into the gloke's face. *FWACK!* The blow drove the gloke backward. It had already been tenderized from waging battle against Pavo. Seefer's high-speed delivery furthered the pain.

Seefer didn't stop. He opened his hand to stop driving the gloke backward. He hovered for an instance, and then pointed his hand away. He closed his fist and soared back toward the other gloke, knocking it back another few feet.

He repeated the process several times, thrusting his arm into the glokes on both sides. Each time, he pushed them back a little further. Any time one tried to swipe at him, Seefer steered himself clear by pointing his fist toward safety.

Seefer quickly got the hang of this gravity band. Despite the stakes, he had fun dodging the swipes and flying into enemy from different trajectories. Down swings, crossovers, and upper-cuts: Seefer mixed it up to keep them retreating.

Finally, the one gloke that barricaded the two from their weapons was thrown back far enough that Pavo could access the goods. "Keep at it!" he yelled.

Seefer continued to pound the creatures with his impacts. The speed at which he moved made it nearly impossible for the monsters to stop him. The effort successfully pushed them back far enough to clear space for Pavo. It also revealed two classroom doors in the process.

"I got them," Pavo signaled. He had Seefer's bag in his hands. He reached in and pulled out a few pint cartons of milk. "Prepare to shield yourself!"

Seefer delivered one quick blow to each then aimed his arm at one of the open classroom doors. He zoomed into the room. The angry glokes crept toward the doorways.

Pavo opened a pint of milk and tossed it at the far gloke's mouth. Bull's eye! Then like a soldier yanking a pin from a grenade, he tore the top off another milk and slam-dunked it into the other gloke's mouth.

When he was certain that both had swallowed what they were given, Pavo grabbed the bag and super-soaker, and ran for cover. He dove into the classroom and shut the door behind him.

The skin on the creatures rippled and quivered. They grew more violent as their reaction worsened. They tried to claw their way into the classroom, but soon after their attempt, they wailed in pain.

SPLURSH!

From inside the classroom, Seefer and Pavo heard the loud sound in the hall outside, like two giant water balloons bursting. They knew it would be messy when they opened the door, but it would be safe.

"I think it sounds grosser when you can't see them pop," Seefer said.

Pavo ignored the comment and held a stern tone. "You need to keep your head level out there, young one."

Seefer adjusted his head unsure why it appeared crooked.

"I mean you need to concentrate!" Pavo dictated. "We could have been killed. We are lucky enough to have a weapon that can easily take these glokes out, but you let it out of your control."

Seefer lowered his head in shame. "Sorry."

"If you want to carry out this mission, you need to act like a soldier," Pavo said.

Seefer held a long pause. He was sheepish to talk after being scolded. He finally let out the words, "But I'm not."

"Not what?"

"A soldier!" he said. "I'm trying to do right by everyone. I didn't ask to be the most sought after kid in...in...the entire blob galaxy!"

Pavo immediately created distance between himself and Seefer. He uneasily paced along the interior wall, tapping his toes and muttering to himself. After a brief moment to himself, he painfully said, "Sorry."

Pavo picked up Seefer's Easton and took it as his own. With it, he walked over to the classroom's door. The narrow window running up the side was useless, being covered in slime. "We need to keep moving and find that friend of yours."

Seefer threw his bag onto his back. He pumped up the super-soaker, preparing it for immediate use. Pavo grabbed the knob of the door and slowly opened it. Seefer aimed the gun into the hallway in case they were greeted by an unexpected visitor.

Pavo swung the door fully open. Seefer looked both ways. Through his night-vision goggles, Seefer saw nothing except oodles of dripping goo covering every surface in the vicinity.

"Do we have to go out there?" Seefer asked.

Pavo shook his head affirmatively and led the way. "They will surely be sending more now that six have not returned. We are no longer safe here."

The pair walked down the hallway, laboring with each step. Every time a foot touched the ground, it suctioned to the layer of ooze. Pulling upward was like having ten extra pounds of weight stuck to each foot.

Seefer looked back at the hallway. *I hope they don't make me clean this up.*

With a few more steps, they made it to the clean floor. Seefer readied his super-soaker as they advanced toward the end of the hall. Pavo stood on alert. He raised his bat in the air and motioned to Seefer to be quiet by laying his finger over his mouth.

The door to the staircase creaked open. There was something coming inside. *No, not more glokes!* Through the night vision goggles, Seefer could see a hint of light shining from outside. It temporarily blurred his vision.

But while those goggles were adjusting, something sprang from the stairs!

18

The figure emerged quickly, a blur to Pavo and Seefer. Pavo took a reactionary swing with his Easton, but missed. In desperation, Seefer pulled the super-soaker trigger and emptied his chamber of milk.

"Ah! What the freck are you doing, Seefer?" shouted Cassy.

"Cassy!"

"I am soaked!" she said.

"You could have been killed," Pavo warned.

"What is this? Milk?" she asked with a disgusted tone.

"Cass, what were you doing?" Seefer asked. "He almost took your head off!"

"I did not realize you would be here. I lost the glokes in the staircase and watched them enter this floor. I was trying to stay behind them. Seefer, I thought you were in the basement."

"I got out, no thanks to you! Where have you been?" Seefer asked with suspicion.

"Tracking. I was trying to follow the glokes to see where they had taken everyone." Cassy was annoyed she had to justify herself. She pointed at Pavo. "What about our friend here? Did you ask him where he went when he left us in the basement?"

"He's been with me," Seefer defended. "We've been making gloke soup." He handed over his goggles so she could see the hallway covered in slime.

"But what about *before* that?" she asked.

"Enough!" Pavo shouted. "No more bickering. The three of us need cohesion."

"Says the one who is suspect," Cassy said.

"Cass, he's right. We are altogether right now. Let's stay that way. In the very least you can rest easy knowing and seeing what everyone is doing. Right?"

"Fine! I will do it for you," Cassy said with a touch of reluctance.

"Thanks."

"But somebody better do something about this wet shirt!" she asserted.

Pavo rolled his eyes. He reached into Seefer's backpack and pulled out another T-shirt.

"Here you are," he said. "I packed extras." He tossed her the small shirt.

She looked at the tag through the goggles and commented. "A small? This might be a little tight." Seefer didn't appreciate that comment.

The three of them stood there looking at the T-shirt,

waiting. Cassy looked up and saw two puzzled faces looking back at her. Seefer said, "Well? We don't have all night."

"Well what?" she responded. "Turn around! I am a lady, you know!"

In dryer clothes, Cassy led Seefer and Pavo outside and across the courtyard. There was a loading zone beneath the cafeteria wing where milk crates were stacked and ready to be returned to the dairy distributor. Adjacent to that was a driveway descending into the custodial courtyard. Much of the outdoor equipment that the custodian was supposed to use was parked there under a tent. The Bilco door that led to the janitor's room was in this courtyard as well.

Cassy led the others to the garbage dumpsters, displeasingly situated in the middle of the rear parking lot. "Climb atop," she instructed as she sprung to the top with two effortless prances.

Seefer jumped and grabbed a hold of the top. His body swung into the side of the dumpster like a pendulum. The impact produced an echoing metallic rumbling. When it was obvious he wouldn't make it up on his own volition, Pavo gave him a boost. When Seefer was safely aboard, Pavo leapt atop the nearby recycling bin.

"Look out there." Cassy pointed away from the school to where the athletic fields resided. The cloud coverage shielded the campus from any moonlight that may have provided visibility. From memory, they knew the baseball and softball fields were off to the left. The stadium that housed football games, soccer matches and track events sat to its right. Beyond them, there were practice fields and open space. Without the use of night-vision, all of it appeared as blackness.

"It's all dark. What exactly are we looking for?" Seefer was puzzled.

"You'll see." Cassy said.

There was a long pause. It was uncomfortably long. Seefer and Pavo continued to watch but having no idea why. "This is madness!" Pavo had enough. "We are sitting here as easy targets. We must move."

"Cass, he's right," Seefer seconded. "Do we have to stand right here?"

"Yes, just wait," she insisted.

Seefer needed to keep peace amongst his allies. He prompted Pavo into not leaving. "Tell her. Tell her about the optimask."

"Optimask?" she asked.

Pavo offered no response. Instead, he climbed off the recycle bin and took steps toward the building.

"Pavo?" Seefer called for his attention, but he wasn't providing it. Seefer tried explaining it himself. "He believes there is a thing called an optimask which is hiding everyone. It's like a big tent that makes everything invisible.

"Oh!" Cassy grinned a mischievous grin. "That

must be what I found leeching off the school's electrical transformer."

Pavo stopped in his tracks. "What makes you think you found the optimask's power supply?" he asked.

"There is a big metal transformer box behind the stadium. Attached to that was a very large metal conduit – one that had not been there before today." Cassy caught Pavo's attention.

"How do you know that it was not there before now?" Pavo asked with disbelief in his tone.

"Because," Cassy said, "unlike you, I have been keeping guard here for the past two months. I scouted the entire campus – the town as a whole – so that when this day came, I could navigate through it like I was reading a map. How long have you been here again?"

Cassy stood atop the dumpster looking down on Pavo with her cold stare. She waited for the answer to her loaded question. Pavo gave none.

Seefer stood next to Cassy, feeling very uncomfortable. He felt it was necessary to break the tension. "A day, right? You've been here a day, Pavo? I'm not sure how it's relevant, but maybe we should just get that out there and move along."

Neither Cassy nor Pavo responded to his comment. He felt like he magnified the awkwardness a few times over.

Cassy remained emotionless, leering at the janitor below. She probably liked that he crawled off his container. Now she could look down on him.

Pavo returned the dirty look and exchanged no words.

Irritated with the standoff between his two allies, Seefer held his hands up in the air and shook his head with annoyance. He wanted everyone to get along. He trusted both of these people with his life, but between them, strangely, they could not trust each other.

Seefer tried again. "Well if you two aren't going to talk to each other, I might as well just–"

BOOM!

"What was that?!" Seefer turned around and saw a blaze of fire and smoke rise from behind the stadium bleachers. Pavo broke off his stare with Cassy and had a look himself. The blast provided a subtle glow over the field, bringing the fields out of darkness.

"I set a small explosive along the cable drawing electricity from the transformer." Cassy looked very pleased by her work.

"Small?" Seefer questioned with shocked tone on his voice.

"It may have been medium-sized."

Pavo quickly hopped back upon the recycle bin to see the commotion. He stared and watched the blaze rise. There was a demanding urgency in his voice when he said, "How close to the transformer did you set the explosive?"

"Far enough to prevent any damage to it," Cassy said.

A gentle humming noise grew from the silence.

"The lights!" Seefer watched the lamps in the parking lot flicker on and provide an amber glow to the loading zone where they stood. The bright white stadium lights were warming up and dumping their bright rays onto the fields all around campus. Seefer missed using his eyes without the aid of the night-vision goggles. He welcomed the chance to pack those away in his backpack.

The outdoor area grew even brighter when the school lit up. Like a set of dominoes, each classroom ticked on from one end to the other, until the entire building was shining.

"I wish you did that earlier, Cass," Seefer said looking around, admiring the light.

"Look!" Cassy pointed to the fields. Beyond the baseball diamonds and the football stadium, there were flashes of white and blue light as large as houses. The patches of color flickered and systematically disappeared to reveal the Science-Mobile Korvus parked in the middle of the grassy field.

"That's the Science-Mobile!" Seefer said.

The back of the van opened up like a box. Ramps led in and out of a curious compartment near the cab. On the flatbed there was a larger tower with a rotating spindle. Drones scurried about trying to figure out why things weren't working.

Seefer, Cassy and Pavo watched diligently to assess as much information as they could while everything was visible.

To the side of the van, a crowd of people stood. They were motionless, lined up in long parallel rows. The crowd was made up of the students and faculty of Harrison. Their immobility had Seefer believing all of the stories of hypnosis and mind-control.

Korvus made an appearance. He stepped out of the van's conspicuous rear compartment. He looked up and around at all the lights. He made steps toward the school. He didn't walk far until he stopped and watched suspiciously.

"Do you think he sees us?" Seefer asked.

"Most definitely," Pavo replied.

Korvus spun around sending his cloak into the air. He pointed and made angry gestures to his crew. Then within a matter of seconds – they were gone!

"What happened?" Seefer said surprised. "Cassy cut the power."

"They must have a backup source," Pavo said. "It will surely not last long. We will have to finish our mission before they run out."

Cassy didn't see the logic. "Why? What will happen then?"

"The perimeter shield will turn off. And when it does, all of those curious and ignorant people standing outside on the road will come running in to help. And they will be in grave danger."

"I don't think we'll have to worry about getting this

over quickly," Seefer said with a lump in his throat.

"Why, Seef?" Cassy asked.

When they looked out in the direction Seefer had been surveying, a sense of doom enveloped them. A pack of ten drones emerged from nothingness, slipping into sight as if they appeared out of thin air. When all were outside of the optimask, they marched toward the school.

Seefer gulped. "It looks like they are bringing the fight to us."

19

BOOM!

"What the heck was that?" Officer Booth climbed up onto his police car to see if it would give him a better vantage point. He, like all of the others out front, could only guess what was happening inside and behind the school.

By now every parent of every student had arrived on scene, being held back by wooden barricades. Police arrived from neighboring towns to assist Camden in keeping order. The explosion sent dismay throughout the crowd. Mothers like Seefer's wallowed for the safety of their sons and daughters. Angry fathers yelled for their release.

"Sounded like an explosion," chimed Police Chief Perry. The raspy-voiced, pot-bellied head of police liked to point out the obvious as a means of always being correct. In this situation, it served as a way to do *something* when the police couldn't do anything.

When Perry accompanied the SWAT team to the

scene, Seefer had just re-entered the building, and his mother was being escorted back to the parents' holding area. After that, nothing occurred outside of the school. They heard some of the ruckus that transpired in the main office and foyer. Glass shattered, furniture smashed and animalistic sounds belted out. They also saw gleaming white lights every now and again from Pavo's light orbs hovering around the school. With all these things happening, there was no way they could get involved.

"We are still waiting for the state to send us a helicopter. No telling what blew up in there." Perry washed his hands of any concern. His stubbornness prevented him from admitting they were helpless while waiting.

"A helicopter? We can't wait any longer. Don't you think we should figure some way around?" Booth was not in any position of authority to be questioning the chief. Due to circumstances, he had become the most knowledgeable on the events of this day.

"I'm open to suggestions," Perry offered.

Stirring arose amongst the crowd. Booth looked to see what the commotion was about. Parents and cops alike were pointing toward the school. One by one, the classroom lights turned back on. In a matter of seconds, the entire school lit up.

In the sky, along a vertical plane in front of the school, huge squares of blue and white light flickered. They popped up in mid-air, about where the perimeter shield was suspected to be. The flickering was fast and mosaic-like, but one could make out the entire shield from the pattern it followed. The flashes went as high as fifty feet above the school and encompassed the entire property line along the ground. Then in a subtle moment, the flashing stopped.

"I think it's off," Booth said.

"What is?" Perry asked.

"The shield they are using," Booth said. "The explosion might have knocked it out." Booth looked back at all of the parents. He spotted Seefer's mom watching with worried tears in her eyes. The cloud of smoke rose high enough to see over the building. For her sake and the sake of the others, Booth felt he had to do something. "Let me go in."

"How do we know it's safe?"

"We don't," Booth said cavalierly. "But somebody has to try it first. I volunteer."

"You're not trained for any tactical engagement," Perry reminded him.

"Then send the SWAT in right after me. We can't stand here while there's a good chance that thing could be off!"

"Fine." Perry motioned over to the SWAT unit. "Mulholland! Have your men escort Officer Booth up to the school." Mulholland, the SWAT team leader, acknowledged the request and readied his team.

Booth ducked under the police line and walked

toward the school. He kept a regular pace. Too quick and he might miss something carelessly. Too slow, and this window may close. The team of four SWAT members followed him with assault rifles ready.

Booth neared the line of the perimeter shield. The grass along its edge was completely flattened. He held his hands out, closed his eyes and took a deep breath. He reached out and – nothing happened. He took a step – nothing happened. He took another. He made it unscathed.

Booth took a few more steps to make sure he was safe. When he found himself still standing and breathing on the other side of the invisible line, relief overwhelmed him. He turned to the others. "I'm in!"

The crowd of onlookers started cheering. This was their moment, too. Authorities would be able to rescue their kids.

The SWAT began their advance. Before they reached the line, the flickering lights returned. White and blue flashes came between Booth and the SWAT members and throughout the entire sky.

"STOP!" Booth yelled. "It came back on!"

The SWAT team didn't acknowledge him and continued to approach. The first one to put his foot near the line was met with a giant force of energy. *B-ZAP!* The shield's power threw him back into the two-team members behind him. The two he knocked over rose to their feet. They tried helping the one on the ground, but the tactical officer would not wake out of his unconscious state.

Mulholland looked at Booth. "What did you do?"

"Nothing! It came back on!" Booth yelled.

"It'd be best if you come back here, officer."

"I'm not sure I would be able to," Booth said. "And with nobody on my side of the fence that can help me, I'm not taking that chance."

Mulholland didn't take to his refusal. "Let's go!" He reached for Booth's hand, but in doing so, crossed the shield. *B-ZAP!* Mulholland flew back twenty feet and landed out cold.

The only hope the folks outside had were now half defeated. No one would have counted on Booth being a factor. Yet there he was, the only cop on the inside. Booth would make sure it mattered for something.

He snapped open the strap on his gun holster and took his weapon in hand. With a tip of the cap to his police chief, he sprinted into the school to save the day.

20

With the revived lighting allowing them to see with full clarity, Seefer and Cassy followed Pavo's instruction on how to deal with their expected visitors. The rear parking lot had spots for more than a hundred cars, but only about fifty of those were used by the faculty and staff. Pavo eyed this area as a suitable battleground.

The drones were halfway in between their camp and the school. They were easy to keep track with the stadium lights reflecting off their mirrored faces.

Pavo dismounted from his perch and started hunting for the best location to carry out this fight. With the Easton gripped firmly in hand, he took practice swings and limbered up, like a boxer waiting for the starting bell.

Seefer and Cassy prepared the super-soaker by filling the chamber with more milk. "Remember," he said to her, "it has no affect on them unless they're outside of their costume."

"Why do I need to know that?" Cassy asked.

"You are going to take this," Seefer said handing her the soaker.

"No," she refused. "What would you use?"

Seefer smiled and pulled out the gravity band from his pants pocket. "I'm itching to put this thing back on."

They leapt off the dumpster and joined Pavo. Cassy strapped the soaker to her back and cracked her knuckles. Seefer shook out his tension. The three of them did their best to ease the nerves that would be needed to take on ten drones at once.

The pack entered the parking lot and slowly walked past a row of empty spaces. Two rows of faculty vehicles stood in between the drones and their targets. The drones split up in to pairs in order to squeeze past the first row of cars. Their short, stout spacesuits made slipping through the cars difficult. As they wedged through, their bulk scratched the paint on most and broke a few side mirrors.

They stayed in smaller groups as they crossed the driving path on the other side of the cars. A few seconds later, they wedged in between the vehicles of the next parking row.

"Now!" Pavo cried out as he leapt onto the hood of a blue sedan parked before him. As he hopped from the hood to the roof, he swung his bat like a windmill knocking one of the drones in the head.

Cassy climbed aboard the station wagon nearest her. Drones flanked her on both sides. From her location, she was able to land precision kicks to the attackers below. Their clumsy suits prevented them from reaching up and grabbing her before she could deliver another blow to their heads.

Seefer allowed a group of three to clear the row of cars nearest to him. The closer they came, the faster he danced. The limbering exercise he performed earlier became a nervous jitter. When they were too close for his comfort, Seefer raised his hands. "Stop!" he commanded. They didn't respond. "Okay, you asked for it!"

Seefer pointed his arm in the direction of the three drones. Unlike the ones in the hallway, they weren't deterred by the gesture. One by one, Seefer clenched a finger – pinky, ring, and then middle – and slowly dropped them into his palm. Then as the pointer finger eased into place, his fist was made. The gravity band activated, and he was off.

Seefer soared toward the trio of drones. He drove his fist into the chest of the one in front, sending it back into the two behind it. Like bowling pins they toppled over.

"Yaaaahooooo!"

Seefer directed his arm upward. The gravity band carried him into the sky. It carried him uncomfortably high. While he was too busy smiling and congratulating himself for his precision strike, he didn't realize how far from the earth he traveled. When he looked down below, he realized he had traveled a hundred feet vertically in a matter of seconds.

Seefer released his fist. When he did, the gravity band powered down, and he immediately began his fall from the sky.

"Help! Help!" he shouted. He flapped his arms vigorously, but the motion didn't stop his descent. He had to quickly think of the other hand gesture that was used to repel.

He pointed at the ground with his index finger, but nothing happened. He tried holding out his palm. Still nothing. He sped through every hand gesture he could think of, but nothing was stopping his fall. He was meters away from impact with the ground.

"Knuckles!" Pavo shouted to Seefer.

Seefer held out his palm toward the ground and bent his knuckles. Instantly, he slowed down until he hovered idly in the air. The bracelet countered the force of gravity.

Seefer's folly led to Pavo's distraction. While he watched Seefer's free fall, four drones tripped him off the blue sedan. They grabbed a hold of each limb and dragged him across the asphalt. Pavo struggled to free his arms from their grasp.

Cassy continued to hold her own. Any time her opponents had the chance to climb closer, she nimbly jumped to the hood of the next car. The vehicles provided an excellent tool for impeding their ability to fight. The drones' exoskeleton suits were too heavy or limited in movement for them to keep up with the lively

Cassy.

Seefer landed safely on his feet and waited for the three he bowled over to rise again. They sure enough did. "Why don't you take off those masks and fight face to face!" he challenged them.

The drones looked at each other, then to Seefer and shook their heads.

"C'mon, guys. Let me see those pretty smiles!" Seefer aimed his arm at them again and tightly closed his fist. The gravity band pulled him toward his target, the drone in the middle. Before reaching it, the drone purposefully fell backward to avoid the strike. The other two were fast enough to grab Seefer by his legs.

This didn't stop the bracelet from propelling forward. The drones held on tightly to Seefer's legs and would not let go. The gravity band had the power to carry all three of them through the air with ease. Seefer's legs, however, were not equipped to deal with the weight pulling on them.

"Get off!" Seefer tried kicking, but the weight was too much for his leg to move. He directed his arm across the parking lot, parallel to the ground. As he sailed over the asphalt, Seefer got as low as possible. The drones dangled closer to the ground than he. When he leveled out at less than two feet above the pavement, their spacesuits scraped hard against the gritty surface.

One of the leeches fell off Seefer's leg and went tumbling into a car. This shifted all the weight hanging off Seefer onto the side the other one clung. The two spiraled uncontrollably. Seefer had to steer away from the ground to prevent injury.

After he created some distance between himself and the ground, he used his free leg to continually knee the enemy in the arm and helmet. The pursuer stayed persistent. It tightened its grasp and climbed up Seefer's body. It hoisted itself up to Seefer's waist level despite his attempts to shake it.

The creature reached up and grabbed Seefer's right arm, the one with the gravity band. Seefer struggled to keep his arm pointed in the direction that he wanted. The drone made it increasingly more difficult to maneuver. With the two of them fighting for control, their flight path grew erratic. Like a house fly, they loop-de-looped around in the sky.

With his free hand, Seefer punched the drone's helmet. *BAM! BAM!* The effort didn't shake it off. Seefer's rattled reflection stared back at him through the mirrored facemask. With a nifty move, Seefer wrapped his free arm onto the other side of the helmet and got the drone into a head-lock. With all of his strength, he pried it off and quickly took hold of the gloke's head between his arm and torso.

The helmet fell through the chilly night sky and crashed onto the asphalt below. The mirrored lens shattered into thousands of pieces as the shell rolled away with the sound of an empty plastic bucket.

The battle on the ground stopped momentarily when attention turned toward the fallen helmet. Cassy, Pavo, and their assailants watched as glass settled across the blacktop. When the drones turned skyward to see where it fell from, the humans used the opportunity to turn the tables.

Pavo unleashed himself from the grips of the drones. "Unhand me!" he yelled. He stood up with his hands raised, ready for a fist fight. The four drones, thrown back from his release, immediately closed in on him.

Cassy kicked an unsuspecting opponent in the helmet, sending it crashing into the broad side of a pickup truck. Its helmet whipped back and broke the cab window.

Another climbed atop the pickup bed, and dived toward Cassy. Cassy was about to be toppled, but Seefer swooped in from nowhere to knock that drone out of Cassy's way.

"Thanks!" she shouted just before she took another one's helmet and smashed it into the car frame.

Seefer still had his adversary's head locked under his armpit as he flew above the cars and parking lot. He tried with all his might to keep the head to his rear, so he would not have to suffer another face-to-face with the species. He was surprised at how effective his head-lock was against the gloke. The blobs he encountered inside the school were much more squishy and malleable, but this one's head had some hardness to it. Also, if Seefer wasn't mistaken, he felt the presence of hair fluttering on the backside of his arm. He didn't dare look; he had enough problems maneuvering with the attacker attached to him.

"You need to get the heck off of me!"

Seefer dove toward the ground, making a fist for added velocity. Before he hit the ground, his hand switched to the knuckled palm. He immediately repelled upward. The sudden jerk in momentum released the gloke's grip and left him tumbling onto the ground.

Seefer looked down to enjoy the reaction of the confused gloke, but when he laid his eyes on the thing he released, he was in for more of a surprise than he expected.

"Hector?"

Seefer's jaw dropped. *How could this be?* He relaxed the fist that carried him upward and immediately began his descent. He had to get a closer look to be sure he wasn't seeing things. As he neared the ground, he validated his first instinct. It was Hector! Seefer laughed to himself at the sight. He looked ridiculous in the spacesuit that was clearly not designed for a human boy.

Hector rose to his feet but made no further movements. He looked skyward with a blank stare covering his face. As Seefer came closer, there was no sign of eagerness or aggressiveness. He simply waited for his moment.

Seefer landed close enough to speak to him. "Hey Hec, what gives? I know you're a jerk and all, but helping the guys that want to destroy the planet?"

Hector gave no response. He continued staring blankly forward. *What was wrong with him?*

Seefer looked around and saw that his friends were in trouble. Cassy was still dodging a quartet of attackers by leaping from one car top to the next, but her stamina was fading. She didn't have many good leaps left.

Pavo had the other five minions going toe-to-toe with him. They had him surrounded in an open area of pavement. Anytime one of them tried to take hold of Pavo, he was able to toss them away.

Seefer wondered how many more of these drones weren't actually glokes. Could they all be students? If they were all kids, how were they so strong and competitive?

Cassy was almost grabbed by the ankle. She narrowly escaped by pulling herself up the side of a student transport van. Seefer saw the strain on her face and the heavy breathing. Forget Hector, he had to help Cassy.

With a turn of his hand, he whisked across a row of cars, zoomed over four drone heads and threw Cassy over his shoulder like a linebacker tackling a runner. He groaned with unexpected pain as he carried her away from danger. Guided by the gravity band, the two ascended atop the school where Seefer gently.

"You're safe." He smiled with confidence.

Cassy shoved him in the arm. "Like heck! Bring me back down there at once!"

"Cass, trust me. You see that shattered helmet down there?" She nodded. "Well, I don't think you saw who was behind the mask."

She looked over the edge of the roof. When she did, she made direct eye contact with Hector who stared right back at her. The four mirror-faces she had tangled with surrounded him. Her stunned expression was shining back at her through each of their lenses.

"That is cheating!" She was furious. "If you are trying to capture someone, you should not have someone else do your dirty work! Now we have no choice but to retreat!"

"Huh?"

Cassy looked at Seefer. "I cannot fight them. They are innocent."

Seefer looked over the edge and sulked. "No, we can fight them. Especially that guy!" He pointed out Hector.

"It is irresponsible. They are under the suggestion of the Halo."

"Fiiiiine!" Seefer said.

She hung her head over the building's ledge. "Pavo!"

Down below, Pavo was in trouble. The spacesuits that were designed to define the blobby shape of the glokes also had the seeming ability to give added strength to those who already had endoskeletons. Every punch that struck Pavo's face weakened him.

Outnumbered five to one, and without a weapon, Pavo could barely take anymore.

Cassy screamed out his name, but he was too consumed to look or respond. He was about to be taken down. Seefer took to the air to go rescue him.

"Seefer! Get back here!" Cassy yelled. He ignored her and dropped from the sky.

Seefer dove quickly and crashed into one of the drones attacking Pavo. Instead of engaging in battle, he quickly leveraged himself into a position where he could torque the helmet off. When he uncovered the being inside, Pavo saw firsthand what he had been fighting.

"A child?" he said in disbelief.

Specifically, it was another one of Seefer's classmates, Jona. Despite being in the midst of a scrum, Jona displayed the same cold demeanor as Hector.

"The humans have found the truth!" Hector barked out a command in an accent that wasn't his own. "Reveal yourselves!"

For a moment, the drones stopped advancing on Pavo. Each of them reached up to their mirror-lensed helmet and twisted it. Once unlocked, they each lifted the helmet up off their head. Pavo couldn't believe his eyes. Every single one of them was a middle-school-aged kid. They looked void of any and all emotion.

Seefer tossed the helmet he pried off Jona. With the kids standing around doing nothing at the moment, he thought it was the perfect time to get away. He reached his hand out to Pavo.

"No!"

"No? Come on. Let's go!" Seefer insisted.

Pavo looked back with the same insistence. "If Korvus resorts to using human children as a weapon, I will not be apart of it. Your only option is to run."

Seefer looked puzzled. *After all this? Giving up now?*

"Now!" Pavo yelled, knocking Seefer out of any thought process he had going. Seefer pointed toward the roof and sailed away.

"Take him!" said the voice speaking through Hector. The kids surrounding Pavo closed in and grabbed him. Pavo gave no resistance. They began their walk toward the athletic fields.

Hector turned to the rest of the henchmen, still donning their helmets. "Find Cepheus and bring him to me!"

The other drones filed into a line and marched into the nearest entrance of the school. Once they entered, Hector stormed off toward the base.

High above the parking lot, Seefer and Cassy perched on the edge of the school roof. From there, they could see the events unfold beneath them. They watched as the zombified servants of Korvus carried Pavo out to the field.

In the distance they could see a billowing tower of

smoke rise from the rear of the stadium. The explosives that Cassy set had caught fire to something nearby. Ash rose but was contained by something above. Once the smoke reached that certain height it was forced to spread outward, forming a black cloud of smoldering dust.

Seefer and Cassy paid little attention to the darkening sky. Wanting nothing more than to end this arduous day, they devised a plan.

"…and I think it will give us the best chance to get inside there without explicitly knocking on the door." Cassy finished her cunning idea.

"Also better than being carted off like some prisoner." Seefer gazed into the distance and watched Pavo being escorted past the football stadium. "Who knows what they'll do to him out there."

"I am still puzzled by Pavo not putting up a fight. That does not help my suspicions of him," Cassy said.

"He didn't want to fight innocent kids, Cass!"

"He did not have a problem using innocent rats for his hide-and-seek project earlier today," she countered.

"Yeah, well, I think beating up kids is where he drew the line." Seefer watched Pavo's captors lead him away. They were getting closer to the optimask area and would soon be completely out of sight. "I wish they would get here sooner. We need to hurry."

"You two aren't going anywhere," said a familiar voice. Seefer and Cassy froze when they heard it and were even more stunned to see him in the flesh. *How did he get here?*

"Officer Booth?" Seefer asked in disbelief.

It was. Booth stood atop the stairs that led to the floors below. He had his gun drawn, but not pointed. He breathed heavily from running around the school looking for signs of life, but missed all the action that led Seefer and Cassy to the roof. He had to approach the situation with suspicion.

"What are you doing up here?" Booth asked.

Seefer frantically gestured to Booth to come to the ledge. "Come here. We were attacked by those guys moments ago. They have the janitor right now!"

Booth hesitated at first but agreed to come to the edge of the roof. He looked out and scanned the seeable campus. He saw nothing. "Son, I don't know what kind of game you're trying to play. Do you realize your mother is worried sick out there?"

"They were just there!" Seefer pleaded for understanding. "They went behind the optimask."

Booth shook his head. "Kid. I have kept a pretty open mind about things today, but you need to stop being so vague. These stories - what are you talking about?"

"He is telling the truth!" Cassy yelled. "The enemy is out there and has a way to conceal their presence. In any moment, they are going to find us here and take us too!"

"Okay. Remind me again who *they* are." Booth

spoke with an unconvinced tone.

"Oh Seefer," Cassy prodded, "show him the gravity band already! Get this moving on!"

Seefer opened his palm toward the ground and crunched his fingers. Slowly his toes rose above the roof as he was lifted several feet into the sky. He hovered above Officer Booth with the hopes this would convince him of all they told him today.

Booth's jaw looked like it was going to unhinge itself the way it dangled from his face. Despite some of the crazy events he had encountered, he could not believe he stood beneath a flying boy.

"So do you believe us now, Officer?" Cassy asked him.

Booth nodded while staring at Seefer hovering above him. The skeptic in him still looked for suspension wires of some type. Seefer floated, spun and twisted in the sky, ruling out any theatrical tricks. This was for real.

Seefer steered himself back down to the roof and rejoined the others. "We need to get out there and put an end to this. When the power came back on, there was a short period of time where we could see exactly where they were."

Booth pointed at Seefer, "What are you waiting for? Can't you fly out there?"

"We are waiting for our hall passes," Cassy said slyly.

"I don't get it," said a confused Booth.

Seefer looked at the staircase and raised a flag. "They're here."

Five mirror-faced suits crept out of the stairwell entrance. Their costumes were scraped and bruised from the scrum in the parking lot, but their posture and stamina seemed refreshed. If it were just children under those helmets, they were under a powerful hypnosis that prevented them from feeling pain.

At first sight of them, Booth drew his weapon and aimed it at the drones. "Halt! Police!" Seefer instinctively planted his foot and turned to Booth. With his palm pointed at Booth's gun, he crunched his fingers. His planted foot stopped him from moving in the opposite direction and instead projected a force outward. It whacked the gun out of Booth's hand and sent it skidding across the rooftop.

"What did you do that for?" Booth shouted.

"They are kids." Seefer informed him. "They're hypnotized and doing the job of blob-like alien creatures."

"Oh," Booth said stunned. "Good to know."

The drones advanced from the stairs and marched across the rooftop toward them. Their boots crunched into the loose asphalt stones lining the roof's surface. Their shuffling feet provided a haunting countdown to an inevitable battle. Cassy held up her dukes, ready for a fistfight. Booth nervously laughed at the situation he found himself in. The laughter was hiding the underlying terror he was feeling.

"So what are we supposed to do?" Booth questioned. He grabbed his nightstick for good measure. Whether they were kids or not, he had to protect himself.

"We have to get those spacesuits off of them. It makes them unnaturally strong." Cassy jumped through the air and tried to take out the one on the left with a pile-drive. The attacker fended her off and tossed her to the ground.

Seefer planted his foot and used the repelling feature of the gravity band to hinder the progression of the pursuers. With each aim and crunch of his hand, he pushed his target back a few feet. Only being able to handle one at a time, he was not able to keep them from advancing, just slow them down.

Cassy climbed to her feet and jumped back into action. The drone that tossed her aside turned its attention to Seefer. She took advantage and leapt onto its back. Interlocking her legs around its chest, she grappled and rode the enemy. Cassy used the leverage to twist off the helmet.

"Helmet is off!" Cassy cried out as she had an 8th grade girl's head in her grasp. Cassy disrobed the girl of her spacesuit.

Seefer's attempts to send back the other four attackers failed. They countered the bursts of force by picking up their pace. Even with Booth's help in tripping some of them up, Seefer couldn't handle the onslaught.

"Officer Booth!" he cried out. "Get ready to turn some heads."

The gang of suits piled onto Seefer and immediately began roughing him up. Booth ran over and pulled one off. He tried going for the helmet, but the drone resisted and thrust its fist into Booth's gut.

The blow knocked the air out of Booth's lungs. As tears streamed down his face from gut-wrenching pain, he could make out the drone preparing for a facial uppercut – and there was nothing he could do to stop it. *BAM!* Booth's lights went out.

Lying under the weight of three brooding attackers, Seefer struggled to keep his head and sides protected. Seefer had seen the bottom of a pig-pile far too often, so he knew how to minimize the damage from kicks and punches. This time he had a way to get out of it.

He flipped over onto his back – usually a death sentence in any fight. Through a seam in the bodies on top of him, he penetrated his banded hand and made a fist. With three people hanging from him, he ascended into the air above the school. He thought about the move that earlier shook off Hector. He contorted his body to repeat it.

Aimed downward, he pointed his fist at the rooftop. With the assistance of gravity he sped toward the surface. The attackers no longer grabbed onto as a means of brutality but held on for their survival.

Within feet of the roof's gravelly layer, Seefer still

hadn't slowed down. He entered into a barrel roll. When the group of four crashed, the drone suits cushioned their fall. Each bumping impact peeled one off until Seefer gently rolled to a stop. Rattled, but not badly injured, Seefer stood and saw the landing track he left behind. All three attackers lied limply on the rooftop.

"Thanks for flying," he quipped.

Seefer quickly scanned the scene. Two enemies remained. One made a fast advance toward him. Booth lied motionless on the ground behind it. To his right, the other drone, the girl from 8th grade was fixing her helmet back on. She was ready to attack him as well. Where was Cassy?

The first drone picked up its speed, then the other one followed in a full out sprint. Seefer couldn't handle the pace of the action and took to the air.

He looked down below and saw the two drones converge at the spot he took off from. He looked over near the building's edge and saw a girl lying on the ground. "Cassy!"

Seefer swooped to her rescue. He landed beside her and quickly turned her over. It wasn't Cassy, though. It was the 8th grade girl.

"What?" Seefer said out loud. Then it made sense to him. When he looked behind him, one drone had the other pinned to the ground. In one swift motion, the drone on top twisted the helmet off the other, revealing a boy from the 8th grade. The drone continued to dismantle the spacesuit leaving the boy in nothing but his school clothes. Despite resisting the assault, the boy never winced nor yelled. He had the complacent hypnotized look on his face like all the others had.

The aggressor stood and with one hand, dragged the boy by the collar. The other hand carried the suit the boy was wearing. It walked over to Seefer and tossed him the spacesuit. "Put this on!" said a garbled voice underneath the mask.

"Cass, I hope that's you in there," Seefer said.

Seefer stared at his reflection in the mirrored lens of the drone helmet before him. In a quick flip, the mask retracted on top. In the shadow of the helmet, Cassy's smiling face showed through. "How did you know?"

Seefer pointed to the 8th grader behind him. "You don't hide your tracks well." Seefer slipped on part of the spacesuit.

"You are going to like this thing, Seefer. It makes you stroooong!" Cassy said with a crazy look of excitement.

"Can't wait," he said. He saw the 8th grader still trying to slip away from Cassy's grip. "What are we going to do with that one?"

"If we lock them up here, it will give us the head start we need. Though, we should get Booth out of here first."

Seefer finished assembling his spacesuit and twisted on the helmet. When it clicked into place, he raised the mirrored visor and said, "Then let's do it."

Cassy left her hypnotized classmates locked and stranded on the roof, as Seefer carried Booth away through the air. They rendezvoused under an oak tree near the parking lot, where Seefer laid Booth's unconscious body down to sleep off his second probable concussion of the day.

"This guy is going to have one heck of a headache tomorrow," he remarked.

"Hopefully that is the worst of his problems." Cassy laughed. "So are you ready?"

"Now or never."

The two unlikely heroes came out of the tree's shadow and into the glow of the amber parking lot lights. With a deep breath, Seefer looked at Cassy in search of confidence. She looked back and gave him a wink. With that, they both lowered their mirrored visors and began their march toward the athletic fields.

21

Graceful they were not. The drone suits that Gliesian glokes use to keep humanoid form were not well suited for beings already of that shape. As Seefer and Cassy hobbled along the trail to the far end of campus, they struggled to keep a fluid and composed motion.

Seefer and Cassy could barely stay upright as they trekked across the Harrison athletic fields. The success of their walk depended highly on their ability to keep each other from falling. *How did the other kids move so well in these things?* Their battle techniques rivaled those of the alien blobs that typically donned the suits. The hypnotic spell they were under must have allowed them to move in ways that Seefer and Cassy are finding it most difficult to do.

If they were wearing normal attire, they would have made it to their destination already. The burden that the costumes present had them still around the 50-yard line of the football field.

"Have you noticed it yet?" Seefer asked Cassy.

"Noticed what?"

"Up ahead. The van. The people. We can see them all. The optimask is down." Seefer pointed out.

"No, it is up. Open your visor."

Seefer slid back the mirrored lens on his helmet. The bottom edge of the visor was like a magic eraser that made everything in Korvus' camp disappear. Seefer fully stowed the visor and looked beyond the stadium. Nothing. Then the realization dawned in his head.

"Whoaaa! This helmet's got X-ray vision!"

"Not quite," Cassy had to correct. "The optimask and these helmets are most likely tuned to the same frequency. When the visor is slid into place, anything behind the optimask can be seen."

"Aliens have the coolest stuff," Seefer marveled.

"I think Pavo might disagree with your word choice." Cassy pointed ahead. She could see Pavo. Glokes restrained him and forced him to kneel before Korvus, who had a most menacing-looking device.

"This is your final chance. Where is Cepheus?" Korvus demanded. He held out a rod with a lime-sized ball at the end of it. He tapped it against his open palm as if to tease his prisoner.

Weary and bruised from fighting Korvus' servants, Pavo no longer put up any resistance to his handling.

He knelt there with a cold dead stare, and had little caution about the consequences of being uncooperative. "Like I told you before, Cepheus is a long way from here."

"You would have us believe you consorted with mere Alpha children?"

Pavo provided no reaction. He allowed Korvus to come to his own conclusions.

"Where did they go?" Korvus squinted his baneful eyes and looked for any clue Pavo's expressions would offer. Pavo returned the icy glare, giving nothing for Korvus to work from. Korvus gave the rod he was holding to the gloke on his right. "Persuasion!"

The gloke shoved the probe into Pavo's mouth. Pavo's eyes widened in shock and desperation. He could not breath. His entire mouth was filled with the end of this torture stick.

A ripple of energy grew outward from Pavo's mouth and blazed its way through his head. His skin undulated and his teeth pulsated from the increasing power generated by the device. If his mouth weren't blocked, he would have surely screamed louder than he ever had. Instead his body convulsed and involuntary functions began to fail. He salivated uncontrollably and bled from his nose.

As the gloke slid a lever from the base to the tip of the wand, the pain grew more unbearable. Pavo tried for air, but had no way to take it in. He choked on his own saliva. He was close to passing out, but hung on.

"That is enough," Korvus said with a satisfied look on his face. The gloke turned off the device and removed it from Pavo's mouth. A stream of saliva poured out with it. Pavo gasped heavily for air. He breathed quickly and deeply, sucking in as much as he could, apparently expecting more punishment.

"I should have rid myself of you long ago," Korvus said with regret. Pavo looked surprised by him saying this. "Oh yes. We knew about you. We knew what you were after. And why."

Pavo laughed at the revelation, despite the pain it cause him to do so. "Then why not kill me long ago?"

"Despite the difference in our ultimate goals, we viewed you as an asset. We have crossed paths before, yes? Did you think we were unaware of your allegiance?"

Pavo remained stone-faced. He didn't let Korvus have the satisfaction of affirmation.

Korvus continued. "We let you believe you were acting in stealth. Your trail was heavily monitored. We always knew which school you were going to next. You did half of our work for us. Your techniques are rudimentary and unnecessarily lengthy, but once you determined that a location was void of Cepheus, you enabled us to relocate our assets elsewhere."

Pavo wrinkled his brow as if he didn't understand. "Why are you letting me know all of this? Now when I *do* find Cepheus, you can be sure that I will be ready for you to come out of the woodwork."

Korvus could not contain his sinister laughter. His eyes squinted like a mouse's and his lips pursed like he chewed on a lemon. "Pavo. Good boy. You are very clever. You try to make me believe you have not found Cepheus?" Korvus shook his finger at Pavo. "Tah tah.

"If you simply had been less distracting today, we may have rolled out of town not noticing it. When we visit one of these schools, we typically take three hours to do a complete scan of the student body. The children are hypnotized to believe they had the best day of school. No one is the wiser. They go home. We move on, searching.

"Not today, though. Our perimeter shield was compromised multiple times. Not by one entity but three. Now, unless we have lost our diligence and missed that you recruited some team members, you have discovered something very unique."

"I have been experimenting with uses for nilpedes," Pavo offered.

"Clever again, janitor. Very clever." Korvus seemed to enjoy seeing Pavo lie his way through the interrogation. "And I suppose it was the nilpedes that set explosives near our power source while you were busy liquefying my minions inside of the school?"

Pavo had no answer. Korvus looked at the sky and saw the smoke cloud grow above their heads. The fire that burned in the adjacent area caught on some brush and trees in the nearby woods. Large flames erupted from the trees.

"You see what you have done?" Korvus prompted Pavo. "This school and everything around it will burn. The smoke will not escape the enclosure. We will all suffocate if the flames do not catch us first."

"How does that help you?"

Korvus curled a knowing smile at his prisoner. He had him completely figured out. "Because you will tell me where Cepheus is before you allow any of these children to be harmed."

A look of concern covered Pavo's face.

"Remember, Pavo, we followed you closely."

The explosives that Cassy set spawned a fire that fully engulfed the plant life around the campus. A pillar of flames rose into the sky and fed a swirling black cloud. No longer could they see the stars or moon. Just darkness – overwhelming, suffocating darkness.

Pavo knew the shield wouldn't last forever. Since Cassy severed the power feed, Korvus' power station ran on reserves. Once those reserves dried up, the shield would disappear, and the smoke would be released. Pavo needed to find an angle.

Pavo spoke. "Let these innocent people go. Let them return to their families. If you do that, I will lead you to Cepheus. Do not endanger their lives!"

Korvus flared his nostrils. "You take me a fool? I know what lies beyond the perimeter shield. If I lift the shield, it would allow anything on the outside to come in. And I am not ready to surrender to such...*terrestrial* authorities. You do not consider me highly."

Something caught Pavo's eye. Behind Korvus, two drones stumbled into view. They descended the hill with a toddlerish stagger. When they reached the outside netting of the optimask, it took them a few tries to find the seam that allowed them passage. Pavo flashed a hint of optimism at the sight of his allies arriving.

Korvus noticed Pavo's eyes following the entrants. He turned and was delighted to see his servants return to base.

"My children," Korvus said with a gleeful smile, "have you found the one I seek?"

Freck! Korvus headed right toward them and with direct questions. *How was a hypnotized child supposed to respond to his mesmerizer?* Seefer and Cassy looked at each other hoping the other would have a brilliant answer, but instead they shook their heads *no* with exaggerated motion.

Korvus threw his hands up in the air and shot Pavo a crazed look of exasperation. "That is why you don't send human children to do the work of skilled Gliesian war-blobs."

Korvus paced around trying to figure out how to get the information he needed. Pavo shot looks over to Cassy and Seefer wondering what kind of plan they had up their sleeve. Without any concrete plan, the only response Seefer could provide was his *I dunno* hand gesture.

Pavo attempted an angle. "Korvus!" He got his

attention. "You cannot hold out much longer. Either we will burn or suffocate, or your power reserves exhaust and you rot in a pathetic jail cell. Release the innocent people and I will present you with Cepheus."

Korvus' lips curled up with contempt. "No. Enough games."

Korvus held out his hands and pointed over to the stand-by army of drone-suited children. Hector stood at the forefront of this group and the first to be summoned. Korvus' spell led Hector away from the pack and over to the area in front of Pavo.

Korvus grabbed the rod back from his gloke minion and stuffed it into Hector's mouth. Hector did not struggle to prevent the act. He fully complied.

"Tell me where Cepheus is, or I will melt this boy's brain!" Korvus threatened.

Pavo fumed and tried to rise off his knees. "Korvus, no!" A pair of glokes forced him back down on the ground.

"Cepheus," Korvus put simply.

"I do not know! Set that boy free! You can do as you wish to me, but leave the innocent out of this."

"Is it not your belief that this Alpha domain is a false existence? It is laughable how much you care for something that you should not even regard as real."

"Let him go!"

"Cepheus first!"

"I cannot tell you." Pavo held his ground despite the

consequences.

"Very well." Korvus fired up the wand in his hand and slid its lever up to the first notch. Waves of pulsating energy emanated from Hector's mouth. Despite being under a veil of hypnotic detachment, signs of pain appeared – tears and wincing grew from his eyes.

Pavo attempted to free himself from the glokes' grip, but he was anchored down too well. Seefer and Cassy stood by anxiously. If they were going to do something, it should have been then, while all attention was on Hector. Not being able to talk for fear of blowing their cover, Cassy walked a few steps ahead. She placed her arm behind her back and motioned Seefer to come.

But he didn't. The blue glow of the torture device reflected off his mirrored helmet. Motionless, he stared at Hector while he was meeting his demise. Cassy turned and saw Seefer doing nothing. He did not acknowledge her presence or even make a natural adjustment in balance. All of his concentration was on Hector's torturing. She whispered in the softest tone, "You cannot possibly hate him that bad?"

WHIIIRRRRRR.

"What the?" Korvus pulled the device out of Hector's mouth and had a look. It was completely powered down. He opened a hatch at the bottom, presumably to access the power source. Smoke rose out of the cavity, indicating that something went awry.

Cassy looked back at Seefer with encouraging glee. Even with her mirrored visor down, Seefer could tell that she was smiling under that reflection on her face.

"Having a problem?" Pavo asked Korvus.

Korvus took two giant steps toward his prisoner, and clubbed his face with the broken wand. Pavo fell to the ground with a mouthful of blood. Despite taking a bruising hit, he cracked a vermillion smile.

"Here!" Korvus yelled out to his cohorts. "Cepheus is here inside this base!"

The glokes, suited and naked alike, began looking around for any signs. Seefer and Cassy copied whatever the other hypnotized kids were doing.

"There is only one way I am going to flush the child out."

Korvus stretched out his clawed hand toward the Science-Mobile. A halo rose up from the top. When the rising mechanism came to a stop, anyone within the optimask could look up and see it – as was the intent of Korvus. The halo started to rotate, swirling the air around it. The motion attracted all eyes.

The crowd of people lined up in rows around the vehicle. Every eye of every student, teacher or staff worker uninterruptedly gazed into the halo.

"Children, allow your eyes to gaze. The halo. Behold. Give yourself in. Free. Your mind is open."

The words lulled the masses into a trance – all except a few. Pavo closed his eyes and looked away.

Seefer and Cassy, who still had their mirrored lenses covering their faces, were protected from the halo's powers. Cassy nudged Seefer to play along like the others surrounding them.

"Now, my children," Korvus called out, "turn your interest to another glow. We are embraced by the warming radiance of the oldest element in the universe – fire. See how it creates both light and dark."

The outside fires mesmerized the students, faculty, and staff of Harrison Middle School. They marveled at the blaze and the clouds of thick black smoke it produced in the sky.

"Yes. Yes, consume it." Korvus reveled in the moment. He scanned the crowd before making his next command. "Cepheus? Are you listening? Reveal yourself. Your time is now. For the sake of the people that stand before me, come forward."

There was no response.

Not getting what he desired, Korvus made good on his threat. "Children, approach the flames."

Every person in the spellbound crowd turned to their left, toward the flame. The rows became lines leading out of the optimask. The first person in every line simultaneously lifted their right leg and moved it forward one step. This was followed by the left leg doing the same. Methodically, the line-leaders repeated the process until a distance of five steps separated them from the next person. Then that person would follow. Then the next.

The robotic march began.

Highly alarmed, Cassy risked being flagged as a dissenter and moved toward Seefer. "Seefer," she spoke quietly through the helmet. Luckily there was enough noise coming from the halo to dampen her voice. "That was you, right? You destroyed the wand?"

Seefer nodded, but never looked her way.

"Can you do the same thing to the halo?" she asked impatiently.

"What do you think I'm trying to do?" he asked snidely. "I need to concentrate."

Cassy left him to work in peace. Seefer locked into the halo high above ground. With his reflective shield protecting his mind from its hypnotic suggestions, he was able to focus his full attention on the mechanics. It was much larger than anything he had dealt with before – faster too. He could not get a fix on the substructure of its mass.

The crowd of people slowly marched to the edge of the optimask. Two teachers located directly in front of the seam reached out and grabbed a side. They walked in opposite directions, pulling open the net that concealed the base. Now, nothing stood in the way of those people and a fiery death.

"Seefer?" pried Cassy.

"Not yet!"

Cassy grew anxious. The front group of people already made it outside. They were now only yards away from the edge of the fires.

"Last chance, Cepheus!" shouted Korvus "These people will perish! Where are you?!"

"HERE!"

Stunned, Korvus turned to the voice coming from one of his henchmen. Showing no fear toward him, the drone stepped forward and pointed at the halo.

"Very well," agreed Korvus. He raised his arm and clawed his fingers. "Return!" The crowd stopped in its tracks, moments before flames would consume the first wave. Every soul turned 180 degrees and began their return to base.

As Korvus lowered his arm, the halo powered down. "Satisfied?" he asked the mysterious person in disguise. "Now, let me have a look at the most wanted child in our realm."

The drone raised its arms and twisted off its helmet. Korvus was stunned. "Cepheus? A girl?"

It was Cassy. She rolled the dice and blew her cover to buy more time. She would have to continue the charade of being Cepheus as long as she could or surely meet imminent doom.

"Last time I checked," she quipped.

"All of the intelligence we have ever gathered on Vela indicated she bore a son," Korvus said.

"Makes for a good disguise, does it not?" Pavo chimed in.

"Scan her!" Korvus demanded of his alien

henchmen. He leered at Cassy with his serpentine eyes. "If you are lying, my dear, you will face a fate far worse than what your friends will be subjected to."

Cassy gulped. Fear, a feeling she rarely felt, overcame her. She watched one alien minion come over to her with a scanner. "What are you doing?" she nervously asked.

"Do not worry. You will not be hurt." Korvus signaled the gloke to begin the scan. "However, if this turns out negative, there will be some pain."

The gloke turned on the device and a flat blue light shined outward at Cassy's eyes. Seefer broke his concentration with the halo to see what they were doing to her. He readied to attack if Cassy was harmed, no matter what consequence it brought. The gloke directed the device up and down, from head to toe. When the light returned back to Cassy's eye level, it zipped away into the scanner.

The gloke read the results tabulated on the screen. It then passed them along to Korvus. He looked over the screen, bringing a look of concern to his face. Beads of sweat appeared on Cassy's brow as she anticipated disaster.

"Disappointing," Korvus said. "While there is no doubt you come from Omega, I expected more ...*irregularities* in your cerebral cortex. I have my doubts about you."

"I was designed to blend in – to be untraceable," Cassy said. She had lied. If that device scanned Seefer, it would take a full minute recording the data it found. Seefer's ability to control gravitational forces came from having a very different brain – one that a standard Gliesian medical scanner would easily detect.

Pavo jumped in, "It is true. Vela took great care in keeping Cepheus a secret."

"Silence! No words from your mouth have a gram of credibility." Korvus lowered his sinister face even with Cassy's. "There is only one way I am ever going to believe you."

Cassy didn't want to respond, but had to know the answer. "And what would that be?"

"Perform." He held up the broken wand. "I know you have found ways of harnessing your ability. Make me believe."

"I cannot."

"TRY!" Korvus yelled with an unexpected ferocity as if his patience had finally expired.

Cassy zipped off the rest of her spacesuit and relaxed her muscles to buy time. She aimed her eyes and hands at the halo above the truck.

Seefer saw what she was doing and continued concentrating on the halo. Now, he had no choice but to destroy it, not only for the sake of his schoolmates, but also for Cassy's well-being.

Cassy pretended to go through the same exercises that she remembered Seefer performing in her living room. She held her hands to her head for dramatic effect.

But with every second that went by, Korvus' eyes squinted tighter from suspicion. "What is it you are actually doing?" he asked.

"I am *trying* to concentrate!"

"Concentrate faster!"

Her breathing increased as more time passed without results. Seefer unflinchingly gazed into the halo. He could sense its entirety and could see where to bend or break it down, but more time was needed due to the mass of the object.

"My tolerance has ceased." Korvus took the dull end of the wand and cracked it across Cassy's face. She squealed and fell to the ground. Never has anyone landed such a blow to her before. The pain was searing.

KRNNNNNKK!

The halo collapsed like an aluminum can being crushed in the palm of someone's hand. All attention turned to the screeching metal as it twisted and warped. Korvus looked back down at Cassy who was still writhing in pain and knew instantly that he was dealing with the wrong person.

"Impostor," he said to himself. He scanned the crowd searching for anyone who could be orchestrating the teardown of the halo. Nobody in the student body fit the bill. They all looked as entranced as they had all day. Korvus turned to his right – Seefer's direction. Standing before him was a boy locked in direct eye contact with him

Seefer removed the space helmet and tossed it to the side. When Korvus looked his way, he stripped the rest of the suit away. Korvus didn't need his scanner – he could tell by the look he received. This child was Cepheus.

"*You* are the one," he said with a not-so-subtle enthusiasm.

Seefer didn't speak. He kept his eyes focused on the enemy before him. His face was full of concentration and his brow showed beads of sweat. He locked in and knew he mustn't let anything stop that. Even the halo collapsing into the ground with a thunderously loud crash didn't shake his focus. When metal shot out and spread debris everywhere, Seefer didn't draw back.

People ran for cover as a shower of shrapnel and silicon rained from the sky. A long steel pipe landed before Pavo.

Cassy groaned as she tried to get to her feet. "Seefer, what are you doing?"

He gave no response, but Korvus added things up. He grabbed Cassy by the hair and pulled her close. "Oh, I see what you are protecting. Let us discuss your options, shall we?"

"Put her down!" Seefer demanded.

"No. Do as *I* say. Cease the theatrics and come with me. No soul will see harm if you comply."

"You lie."

Korvus rolled his eyes in contempt. "Dealing with

children is unbearable. You do not want to cooperate. So be it!" Korvus raised his hand and prepared to strike Cassy. As his fist swung down toward her head, something stopped it, but nothing was there.

"Let her go!"

Korvus tried to budge his arm downward, but it wouldn't move. It was held in mid-air by an invisible force. "I can still crack her neck with one arm."

Korvus motioned to do so, but was instantly thrown back ten meters. His body slammed hard against the ground and the air inside him escaped with a grunt. He attempted to pick himself up but immediately collapsed.

Seefer took measures to keep him down. While still in tune with the parts that made up the halo, he conjured a cyclonic force that swept the debris in to the air above Korvus. Pieces of metal and electronics swirled together and formed a spherical cluster. When Seefer intentionally ceased his focus, the material fell to the ground. Korvus' own technology buried him.

The glokes holding Pavo captive turned their attention toward their leader's apparent demise. Communicating to each other in muffled words, they discussed their next move. In their moment of confusion, Pavo slipped his bonded wrists under his legs and grabbed the pipe he had his eyes on. The pipe made for a handsome weapon. It was long enough to wield like a bo staff, but carried the weight of a deadly bludgeon.

Despite being blobs of jelly, heavy impacts could

concuss a gloke's central nervous system, knocking them out cold. Knowing this, Pavo made one powerful swipe across the back of the turned glokes' heads, splashing them to the grassy ground.

Glokes from inside the vehicle and ones intermingled throughout the crowd came running out. Angry or threatened by Korvus' defeat, they rushed Seefer.

"Watch out!" Cassy yelled out to him. She pulled herself upright and hobbled over to his aid. Even though she was in busted shape, she upheld her duty to protect her friend.

Protection was something Seefer didn't need at the moment. His eyes glossed over as if he were in another state of mind. From his vantage point, he could sense beyond what his eyes allowed. All of the dozens of alien attackers were in his scope of *vision* and – more importantly – in his range for countermeasure.

One by one, glokes flew up into the air like they were being yanked by snare traps. Not one came close enough to even threaten a bruise on Seefer, though. High up in the air, against the shell of the optimask, the glokes stayed pressed against the inner surface. They were confused, frightened even. Seefer had trouble making his next move.

Cassy tilted her head high and marveled at the site of these blobby masses hovering above. The soldier in her gave her the words that she relayed to Seefer. She grabbed him softly by the hand and whispered, "Drop them."

In a simple break of concentration, Seefer released control of the force that held the glokes afloat. Like gelatin falling through the air, they tumbled downward until splattering onto the ground. Although they were disfigured and spread out, they stayed intact like giant membrane patties.

Seefer took a deep breath of relief. He came out of his subconscious state and set his eyes on his real surroundings. He had made quite a mess!

Cassy grabbed hold of him with a giant bear hug. "Seefer! You did awesome!" Seefer looked concerned and disgusted with himself.

"What is wrong?" Cassy asked.

"Korvus. I think I may have killed him," he replied.

"Seef, he would have killed all of us if you had not stopped him. You are a hero."

Pavo rejoined his comrades who were putting themselves back together. "See, young one? All you needed was the right motivation."

"Yeah, nothing to it." Seefer said somberly.

"What are we going to do with them?" Cassy asked about the beaten glokes.

"This quiet will not last," Pavo said, looking to Seefer. "The glokes will reform and rise again unless – I think you know what we need to do. We cannot allow anyone to see them here once we turn off the perimeter shield. It is for everyone's safety."

Seefer understood. He retrieved the spacesuit he wore into the optimask and reached deep into the leg. "I brought some just in case." He pulled out a container of milk he had stowed in the suit.

Pavo smiled. "Be mighty."

Acting quickly, the three avengers subjected the fallen glokes to small doses of milk, and then sprinted back for cover inside the remains of the Science-Mobile. When they heard the explosion of milky insides splatter against the steel siding of the truck, they knew it was clear to exit.

"Whoa! That smell!" Seefer remarked. "It's like ten times worse."

"It is ten times the discharge," Pavo noted.

"And this was the only way of terminating these blobs?" Cassy asked as she minded her steps, careful not to slosh into any goop.

"The only way that did not involve explosives, fire or radiation – all methods that would have harmed everyone else under this dome," informed Pavo.

Seefer walked near the groups of students and teachers wanting to help them out of their gooey covering. Upon closer encounter, he noticed they still had the dazed and confused looks on their faces. "Pavo! Why aren't they back to normal? The halo is destroyed."

Pavo shot a look of curiosity. He hadn't thought of it earlier, but those people should be bustling around wondering how they got out there. "That is odd. A halo provides a connection between one's mind and a subject's. Destroying the halo does not necessarily break a hypnotic suggestion. Only the person who created the suggestion can do that, but you took care of that problem."

"Right…" Seefer sounded very unsure of himself. "So the only way that everyone would snap out of it would be if…"

"Korvus was dead."

Shreds of doubt overcame their faces. They hurried over to the pile of rubble that buried Korvus and peeled back layers of extruded metal and plating. Cassy saw something immediately. His cape! "I got him." She reached in and pulled as hard as she could. With a strong tug she pulled him from the wreckage. She did not expect the result of her retrieval.

Seefer was aghast. "Is that his skin?"

Disgusted, Cassy threw what she had in her hand down on the ground. What she had pulled out certainly appeared to be skin. Underneath the Magnificent's costume was a leathery and wrinkled hide that sort of resembled the Korvus whose face they'd grown familiar with.

"My sums." Pavo grew worried. "He was – is one."

"One what?" Seefer asked fearfully. He picked up the *skin* and inspected it more closely. On the outside, it resembled a very well-made Halloween costume, with real hair and blemishes. On the inside, there was a mesh of graphite, metal and gold – a complex combination of armor and electronics. "He – *It?* – was a gloke?"

The ground rumbled below their feet. "Move!" Cassy yelled. The three of them backed away from the site. Pieces of metal in the giant pile shifted around and spread out.

"What's happening?"

"I think it is safe to say Korvus is still under there somewhere." Pavo seemed to state the obvious. "We need to back up."

Seefer and Cassy followed Pavo's advice as they watched the ground underneath the debris fall apart. A sinkhole developed, swallowing the remains of the halo and all of the other garbage that once buried Korvus.

The quake stopped. Seefer looked down into the deep black sinkhole and wondered where everything went.

"I would not get too close, young one," Pavo warned. "I have only seen one thing burrow through bedrock like that. No, Korvus is no gloke, but gigaverm. Similar, but deadlier."

"How?"

Pavo quickly uttered, "Sentient and malleable like the glokes, but faster, smarter and stronger."

"Oh, is that all?" Seefer said.

"No, they can also gnaw through concrete, rock or metal like you would a cracker."

"Ohhhh." A panicked look overtook Seefer's face.

Cassy continued to look for any sign of Korvus. "Is

there any chance he left?"

Pavo regretfully shook his head from side to side. "He has a mission to complete. His skin suit is damaged. He needs time to heal before finishing it. We should leave now."

The three of them backed away from the hole and headed in the direction of the school. They did not go far before the ground shook again. The earth before them liquefied and sunk into the ground. Chunks of sod and rock fell into a giant forming sinkhole.

Cassy gasped. "Too late."

An enormous black worm rose from the hole and reached toward the sky. The creature was darker than any of the glokes they encountered and bigger too. It had small yellow serpentine eyes and strands of silvery hair, which oddly resembled the human version of Korvus. As the figure stretched out thinly from the hole, parts of its body took a more solid shape. When it completely climbed out from the depths of the earth, it settled into a pillar-like form, towering over the trio below.

They stood frozen, waiting for it to make an offensive move. It remained still to produce words the humans could hear telepathically. "If you will not come peacefully, I will take you forcefully."

Seefer was overtaken by a moment of courage or possibly insanity and stepped forward in front of his friends. "I'd like to see you try, Korvus!" He looked back at Cassy with a grin. She returned his look with a frightful expression.

"So be it!" Korvus twisted his upper body as if it were gaining the momentum of a whip.

Seefer turned to Pavo. "Get the milk ready!"

"Young one, we are out," Pavo dreadfully informed him.

"Oh crud."

Seefer looked back at Korvus before he lunged the top of his wormy body toward him. A mouth ripped open on his head revealing rows of blunt teeth. Seefer jumped clear of the gigaverm's attempt to swallow him, but Cassy was not so lucky. His creature form knocked her backward, and she skidded across the topsoil. Her body went over the edge of the original sinkhole.

"Cassy!" Seefer shouted. She was gone. Into the depths of the ground below.

The gigaverm recoiled and attempted another strike. Both Seefer and Pavo successfully dodged his effort.

"I am okay!" Cassy shouted from inside the hole. She hung onto a root poking out from inside the hole.

"We're coming!" Seefer shouted. He ran toward her, forgetting he was also being pursued.

"No," Pavo stopped him. "Run! Fast! I will save your friend."

"Somebody! Now!" Cassy screamed.

"Go!" Pavo insisted to Seefer. He obeyed and took off toward the school. He jumped clear of another swipe from Korvus before entering into a full sprint that led him out of the optimask.

Pavo leapt to Cassy's aid. He slid over to the edge of the sinkhole, causing more soil to collapse into the hole. He almost tumbled in himself, but was able to stay on steady ground. He reached his hand down to Cassy. "Take my hand!"

If there was any chance Pavo had to get her out of the way, it was now. One loose grip and she would fall into the abyss. Under the circumstances, she had no other options. She released one hand and reached for Pavo. When their fingers interlocked in a tight grip, Pavo pulled her to safety.

"Thank you, I owe you," she said with genuineness. "Where is Seefer?"

Pavo, possibly regretting that he failed to protect Seefer for the life of someone who was not the key to humanity's survival, simply stood and pointed toward the school. With the brush fire raging on, all they could see was a cloud of smoke.

"How can we help him?"

Pavo looked at the thick black ceiling that was consuming everything under the perimeter shield. "We need to help him breathe."

Seefer ran for his life, but would not be able to continue his pace without better air. He had to run on the ground because the sky was too hot and formidable. His gravity band was useless at the moment. He had to make it to the school before the smoke completely filled the dome.

Korvus stayed in close pursuit, making exacting strikes at his target. Seefer realized that by moving in erratic diagonal patterns, Korvus was unable to achieve the desirable angle to capture him. The gigaverm tried to swallow Seefer whole, but taking care not to rough him up with his stone-like teeth.

He let out a hacking cough. His lungs burned from breathing in trace amounts of ash and smoke. Even though it was worse above, breathing conditions were far from ideal on the ground.

Seefer somehow cleared the athletic fields unscathed. He knew it wasn't much further until he reached the school. He thought there could be a room somewhere inside that would provide a pocket of clean air. He longed for a deep breath of oxygen.

Something up ahead ran toward him. Five shadows appeared to be running from the school and closing in on Seefer. He couldn't tell what they were. With a giant alien worm chasing him from behind, Seefer took his chances with the unknown ahead.

In an instance, the shadow materialized through swirls of grey – it was the 8th grade girl they locked on the roof earlier. She tried to take Seefer out by the ankles, but he was nimble enough to hop over her. He was getting quite good at dodging trouble. As soon as he regained his footing, he was almost knocked off them again, this time by the 8th grade boy.

These distractions nearly cost him. If he hadn't

turned at the very moment, he wouldn't have been able to leap away from the Korvus' latest strike.

The still-hypnotized students were costing him time he didn't have. If he couldn't get fresh air soon, he'd pass out.

Got to use the gravity band. Now or never. Seefer raised his arm and pointed directly to the school. He crossed the fingers of his other hand in hopes he didn't shoot straight into a car or light post. Then with the deepest breath he could muster, he clenched his fist and shot out, leaving the attacking students and Korvus behind.

Speeding through a blinding smoke cloud, Seefer struggled to keep his eyes open. The smoke might as well have been a blazing flame the way it seared his unprotected corneas, but if he closed his eyelids, he could end up like a pancake on the school exterior.

"Aaaargh. Can't see!" he yelled to himself.

But then an amber glow poked through the haze. He could see the lights from the school. Erring on the side of caution he slowed himself down and ran the rest of the way.

He swung open the rear door that led into the gymnasium. Upon entering, he quickly closed himself in. He took a deep breath, but instantly went into a coughing fit. The inside of the school wasn't as bad as outside, but it was still filled with a thin smoky haze.

"Got to find air!" He held his T-shirt over his mouth and walked deeper into the gym. He trampled over a row of folding chairs that remained untouched from the morning's assembly. *Where can I go?*

The building began to shake. Seefer knew his time was short. He escaped the gymnasium into the hallway as the back wall of the school came crumbling down. Korvus was in hot pursuit and nothing stood in his way.

Seefer could hear the crumbling of brick and mortar from behind him. He forced himself to think and act faster. *A classroom?* It wouldn't give him any breathing relief – or concealment for that matter. *The basement?* It wouldn't be as smoky, but if Korvus continued to destroy the school, he'd be buried. *Upstairs? What's upstairs?* More smoke, no doubt. *The cafeteria!* The cooler in the kitchen should be sealed and its metal walls might provide some protection!

Time was up. He had to go. He darted through the corridor and into the stairwell. Seefer could hear the gigaverm bulldozing its way to the front of the building, taking out the entire main office and hallway.

Seefer ascended the stairs as quickly as he could, skipping over steps to reach the top faster. The higher he climbed, the thicker the smoke got. He didn't care. He was close.

When he reached the top, he tried to pull open the door, but it wouldn't budge. His vision was too obscured to see what was getting in the way. He gave it another tug, but it would not open. His sense of urgency increased when he heard the doorway being plowed down by the gigaverm. Rubble caved into the stairwell, collapsing half a flight of stairs.

As Korvus destroyed the outer wall, smoke flowed outside making it easier to see at the top of the stairs. Seefer cracked his eyes open and could see his problem. The belt he looped around the handles was still in place. "Idiot!" He quickly undid the buckle and entered the second floor hallway.

Without a breath, he sprinted toward the cafeteria. Adrenaline coursing through his veins supplanted any need for oxygen. Before the worm of destruction made it onto the second floor, Seefer had already made it into the lunchroom.

"Almost there!" he coached himself on. He tried to take a deep breath under his T-shirt, but the amount of filth and soot on it made it a lousy filter for the smoke. He neared unconsciousness, but his ambition carried him forward. He had to make it a little further.

He barreled through the kitchen door and fell flat out onto the tile floor. The cool tiles were the perfect remedy for his overheated skin. He had to convince himself that they weren't enough. He had to get to the cooler. Seefer dragged himself across that floor until he reached the large metal refrigerator. Finally, relief!

Inside the cooler, there wasn't a hint of smoke. Seefer took long deep breaths and relished in the cool oxygen filling his lungs. The sudden change of climate was intoxicating. Instead of hot smoldering smoke filling his lungs, he was now sucking in ice-cold pureness.

After his body had time to adjust to the change, his mind went back to thinking of the danger pursuing him.

Outside the cooler's exterior, pots and pans began to shake. Sounds of metal clanging and cookware shattering penetrated the dense walls. The gigaverm was out there, looking, over-turning everything it could until it found what it was looking for.

Seefer stood on edge. He felt little comfort by the cooler's ability to keep him safe. After all, one simple pull of the handle would be all it takes to enter. *Could Korvus do that in his current form?*

A voice came from somewhere, if not all around. "You have no place else to go." It was Korvus. "It would be best if you come out."

"No way!" Seefer shouted back. Korvus hadn't shown the ability to open a door without plowing it over; and moreover, Seefer was not ready to go back into the fire.

"So be it."

THUNK!

Korvus rammed the cooler door, shaking everything on the inside. Food products fell from their shelves and stacked boxes toppled over. The impact left a large imprint on the inside of the door.

"I hope that hurt!" Seefer yelled at him.

More noise came from outside, like he was burrowing again. *Was he leaving? Hopefully injured from that ram?* But the questions soon were answered negatively. The burrowing noise got louder and it moved to underneath the cooler.

Seefer looked below him, ready for any attack to come his way. The building started to give way as the beast wrecked through the layers of concrete and steel supporting the rest of the building. The cooler began rocking and Seefer was tossed to the side by the force.

Suddenly, all gravity disappeared. Seefer floated in mid-air. He was falling. An instance later, gravity returned in a sudden crash. Everything inside the refrigerator flew into different areas. In the midst of the chaos, the box lost power and not a trace of light leaked in from outside. Inside, Seefer lied amongst the darkness and scattered debris waiting for what would come next.

He heard more destructive noises from outside as Korvus burrowed his way out from underneath the rubble. Once those digging noises ceased, there was quiet.

Seefer could not see. The darkness was uncomfortable, but was something he could tolerate when the alternative was smoke-filled air. He knew it wouldn't be long, though, until he'd be forced back out. He felt the area around him looking for something, anything he could use if his shelter should be dismantled.

"Oh sweet mercy!" Seefer exclaimed. He found something that he could use against Korvus. His hand gripped it tightly as he waited for the enemy to strike.

BAM! The cooler shook as he tried to get in. *BAM!* The next hit weakened its structure. The walls wobbled and caused loud creaking noises along the edges. Slivers of light shined through tiny seams in the exterior.

BAM! One last strike was all that was needed to break the cooler apart. The walls fell out from the center and the ceiling flew off far away. Seefer took one last refreshing breath before smoke filled the air around him. All of his shelter taken away, he curled himself up into a ball. He hid his secret weapon underneath his body.

"Why do you make it so hard on yourself, boy?" Korvus spoke telepathically. "Had you come easily, your friends would at least have a place to learn their archaic knowledge."

Seefer gave no response. He stayed silent and hunched, appearing as a boy cowering in terror.

"So be it. You will ride back to Omega as a passenger in my gizzard." The giant gigaverm grew its mouth open wide and bellowed out a loud roar. The ground shook. All smoke in the immediate area blew away with its exhalation.

Seefer peeked an eye up at the creature to see what it would do. Korvus lifted his head in the air and elongated his neck. In one fluid motion, he swooped down to swallow Seefer whole.

Before the gaping mouth reached the ground, Seefer stood up straight as an arrow holding his salvation up high – a gallon of Grade A vitamin-D-enriched whole milk. "I've got something you can wash me down with!"

Korvus' gained too much momentum to reverse his motion. Even though his beady yellow eyes caught sight of the deadly dairy poison, he could do nothing to stop his swift descent onto and over Seefer. The alien mouth encompassed him and the gallon of milk he held.

When Korvus realized what he had done, he writhed in agony. His bestial form convulsed for survival and ejected what it had swallowed. With an exaggerated motion, he spit out Seefer, sending him and the gallon of milk he held flying onto a bed of crumbled brick and concrete.

Seefer winced and grabbed his thigh tightly. "My leg!" he wailed. It was broken. There was blood, but he wasn't sure where it came from. Suddenly riding passenger inside an alien didn't seem so bad.

Korvus slithered toward him. Seefer was helpless to do anything. "Foolish thing to do, human. You must keep in mind that I only need to take you back alive. There is plenty of pain that I can afflict upon you before you even come close to death."

Seefer sat upright holding the jug of milk in his hand. "Don't come any closer!"

"It would take more than splashing some milk on me to stop me." Korvus warned.

Seefer smiled. "Oh? And what would happen if you swallowed this all?"

"That will not happen."

"Won't it?" Seefer turned the jug over and pointed the spout toward the ground. Only a few drops trickled out onto the rocks below.

A fearful expression overcame the face of the amorphous gigaverm beast. The realization that a gallon of milk was flowing through its system suddenly made it viciously upset. It sneered then twitched. A few moments later, its entire body began to seizure. In one last effort to avenge itself, it darted toward Seefer.

Seefer stood his ground as Korvus sped his way. He held strong, but with every yard closer it got, the more concerned he grew. But then –

SPLURSH!

Korvus exploded in a magnificent creamsicle-colored mess. The goop spread wide and far covering everything within a thirty-meter radius, including Seefer.

Seefer hardly minded. He had seen enough of it today, that it didn't faze him. "I'm going to miss this," he muttered to himself.

Broken in probably more places than one, he couldn't move. He looked around and was surrounded by the glow of orange flames and swirling smoke. He tried to enjoy the hellish scenery as he waited for help to arrive. Maybe it was either exhaustion setting in or a lack of oxygen from the smoke, but sleep became irresistible. Despite all of the excitement and the increased levels of adrenaline, it only took two bobs of his head before he passed out against the crumbled wall beside him.

22

Seefer lay motionless against the rocks. His battle-worn body needed every wink it was getting. Even when the relief of a cool November breeze whisked across his nose, the flaring of his nostrils was the only movement he made.

"He is over here!"

Seefer recognized that ever-jubilant voice piercing through the silence. He lifted an eyelid to see Cassy skipping over debris in order to reach him. She enthusiastically waved to Pavo, who searched another area of the destroyed building.

"Seefer! You are alive!"

"I don't feel like it," he said while realizing he could breath freely again. "No smoke."

"Pavo and I took care of the Science-Mobile. When the shield went down, the smoke was free to dissipate."

"What about the people?" Seefer asked.

"The trance is broken. They are all starting to regain consciousness," she said. "Come. We have to get you out of this mess." She extended her hand, to which Seefer grabbed. When she tried to hoist him up, he growled.

"No! I can't. It's broken!" He touched his leg delicately.

"Time to be a man, child. Quickly," Pavo said as he neared. He looked at the lay of the area. The crumbled cement and brick was layered with ooze then covered with black ash on top of that. Smoke cleared out fast. Without a building standing in the way, the lights and sounds of the street were now perceptible. "Where is Korvus?"

"I blew him up. Did you doubt it?"

Pavo noted the blackened goop sticking to the bottom of his boot. "Once we saw your schoolmates coming out of their trance, we knew you must have done something right." Pavo grinned. "Either that or he swallowed you up and took you back to Omega."

"Close," Seefer grunted as he shifted his weight. He was in serious pain.

Cassy tried to level with him. "Seefer, I know it hurts, but to ensure nobody ever finds you again, we have to leave before those authorities figure out the shield is down."

"I'm not going anywhere until I see my mom."

"We can come back for her!" she said.

"Too late," Pavo said. "We have been seen."

They looked at the parking lot and saw a crowd of

hundreds walking toward the demolished school. Faces donned looks of confusion, sadness and awe. As the students and teachers of Harrison Middle School slowly regained their consciousness, most were trying to figure out how the sight before them came to be.

A whipping noise approached from the distance. The clearing smoke swirled and wind picked up. A helicopter appeared over the distant trees shining a night-sun on the ground below, scanning for signs of life. When the spotlight landed on the crowd of people, the pilots kept it focused there.

Pavo analyzed the scene and came up with a different solution. "We cannot run. Not now. We must blend in." He knelt next to Seefer and looked him sincerely in the eye. "We, the three of us, have to maintain that we knew nothing about the on goings of today. No one can know. We must act like the others – clueless and unknowing. Can you do that?"

"But people saw me. Out front. There was a cop, Officer Booth." Seefer looked over his shoulder at the spot where he left him. "Is he there?"

"Never mind that! You keep to this plan and we will figure it out later." Pavo turned to Cassy. "You too."

"Pretending is all I do around here," she said.

"Will you comply?" Pavo asked Seefer.

"Do I get to stay?"

Pavo rolled his eyes but then gave a half-hearted affirmative nod.

"Then okay," Seefer agreed.

Pavo grabbed him by the arm and lifted Seefer onto his feet. A jolt of pain shot up from Seefer's leg as the broken bones clicked together. "Aaargh, careful!" he shouted.

They looked over their shoulders, to the street, and could see an approaching mob of cops and parents. This prompted them to move. Pavo picked Seefer up and carried him over to the crowd of students. Cassy followed close behind, preparing the charades she would be playing out in a few moments.

The three mixed into the crowd of befuddled students and teachers. Principal Witik was near the front trying to calm a large group of upset children. Teachers counted heads of students they were supposed to have in their class. Seefer spotted Mrs. Cody and pointed her out to Pavo.

"I will need to take back the gravity band," stated Pavo.

"Oh man! Do I have to?"

"Quickly!"

Seefer handed it over to Pavo, who discreetly placed it in his pocket. He then carried Seefer over to his teacher's group and set him on the ground. The throbbing pain in his leg was too much for him to stand on his own. Pavo moved Cassy closer to Seefer and made him lean on her shoulder. "Help him out until he is given medical attention."

"You are not staying here?" she asked with

suspicion.

"That would not be realistic. I am just a lowly janitor." Pavo whispered with a wink. "I will be close by. Remember, you cannot remember."

Pavo patted them each on their shoulders then weaved his way into the crowd of many. He disappeared into the masses.

Before they could dawn on his exit any longer, they heard their names called out. "Seefer! Cassy! Thank goodness." It was Mrs. Cody. She looked disheveled from the crazy day. "I'm so glad I found you. We've got everyone now." She spoke more quietly so only the two of them could hear. "You don't happen to remember anything do you?"

Seefer and Cassy raised their eyebrows with a fake innocence. They looked at each other, then Mrs. Cody and shook their heads *no*.

"Didn't think so. That's fantastic."

Seefer adjusted himself to take the weight off his bad leg. He used Cassy's shoulder as a crutch. She put her hand on top of his and gave him a "hang in there."

Seefer saw Hector amongst his classmates. He wondered how his head was feeling after being Korvus' puppet for the day. From his appearance, he looked like he had been sent through the ringer. *I wonder if he'll need that extra pair of undies after a day like today?*

Police circled the remains of the school and many were within close range to the student body. Some scoped out the surrounding areas with flood lamps, probably looking for any hostiles. When searching the perimeter, one cop uncovered Officer Booth and brought him to his feet.

Booth was dazed but tried his best to answer questions that the other cop was giving him. Seefer didn't know exactly what was being said, but he feared how Booth's inevitable report would somehow come back to him.

"Look." Cassy nudged him to look back at the incoming crowd. Parents flooded into the rear parking lot. All were scanning, yelling and calling out for their loved ones. In the confusion of a hundred voices, only one stood out.

"Seefer!" His mom's voice cried out and seemed to transcend above all others. Seefer was never happier to hear her.

"Mom!" he yelled out. He tried to walk to her, but stumbled immediately. Cassy quickly caught him and threw his arm around her neck. Together, the two hobbled toward his mom.

"Seefer!" she cried out again. "Seefer Elliot!"

"Over here!" Seefer waved enthusiastically. Finally his mom picked him out of the crowd and ran over. She pushed through some folks standing in her way, determined to keep Seefer in her sights the whole time.

When she got to him, she grabbed a hold of him and lifted him free of Cassy's support. He yelled out, "Owwwww! Mom!" She quickly put him back down which made him growl in pain. "Mom, easy!"

"Look at you, honey. Oh baby. What happened to you? You're a mess! What's wrong?" She blurted out sentences at a mile a minute.

"Mom," he grabbed a hold of her hands, "I'm alright. I'm a little roughed up." He looked at Cassy for some indication on what else he could say. She shrugged her shoulders.

"Who is this?"

"Cassy," Seefer said. "My friend." Cassy smiled in appreciation of that recognition.

Mom nodded in Cassy's direction as to greet her, but her pleasantry was short. She turned to Seefer for answers. "So what happened to you, honey?"

Seefer retraced all of the day's events in his head. More than the physical adventures of soaring through the skies above Harrison Middle School and battling extraterrestrials was the information he obtained from Pavo and Cassy. For reasons that were not fully clear to him yet, he was a wanted commodity. An entire race of aliens regarded him as their salvation. Their survival would mean the end of humanity.

Those aspects still seemed like fantasy. The heavy thoughts that occupied his mind were the ones that involved his mother – or mothers. In one day, his outlook on life changed dramatically. He had so many questions, and the only person who he could get answers from was a complete stranger. Now his familiar mother, mom, knelt before him and he found himself asking those same questions again. *Where did I come from? Who is my father? Did you realize aliens from another universe would someday come to find me? What would her answers be?*

The words Pavo last said to him popped back into his brain. "Remember, you cannot remember." *Why?* Even though he asked himself that question, he knew. Discretion was for everyone's protection. The less people knew, the less likely anyone would find him again. And if nobody finds him, then nobody will get hurt. He didn't want that, especially for the ones he loved.

His thoughts trailed. His mom asked him again. "Seef? What is it? You can tell me."

Seefer looked into his mother's eyes, her warm caring eyes, and told her the only thing he thought he could. "I…I don't remember."

Seefer Elliot will return in:

SEEFER ELLIOT
AND THE DARKNESS WITHIN

Look for it at your favorite bookstore!

PAT MALLON grew up loving comic books, sugary cereal, and tuna fish sandwiches. He went to school, traveled a bit and fell in love with a girl. He now resides in New England with his wife and their three children. He spends his time illustrating books for children, a webcomic for older kids (who some call 'adults'), and enjoying comics, cereal and tuna.